# CALEB STAKER

Copyright © 2023 by Juicebox Studios LLC
All rights reserved.
This is a work of fiction. Names, characters, places, and incidents are a product of the author's imagination or are used fictitiously and should not be construed as real. Any resemblance to actual events, locales, organizations, or persons, living or dead, is entirely coincidental.
No part of this publication may be reproduced, or stored in a retrieval system, or transmitted in any form of by any means, electronic, mechanical, photocopying, recording, or otherwise, without written permission of the publisher. For information regarding permission, write to Juicebox Studios or Caleb Staker.

Cover drawn and inked by Aaron Conley based on characters and concept designed by Caleb Staker.
Art direction and color done by Caleb Staker.
Interior illustrations drawn and inked by Aaron Conley. Art directed by Caleb Staker.

# SOGGY TOWN

# CALEB STAKER

Dedicated to everyone in the depths of darkness:
You are not alone.

# Introduction

When I was in high school I would draw in my notebooks this recurring image I had in my mind. It was of a blue hairy monster, a bigfoot sort of creature that had pulled off its human skin suit and left it draped over a tree branch as it walked away. I was trying to draw how I felt—like some type of monster, uncomfortable in my own skin.

I think all of us feel or have felt that way before. Awkward, and not quite sure where we belong. Throw in all the demands of life and expectations from society, family, and ourselves, and these uncomfortable insecure feelings become the perfect recipe for anxiety and depression—something I ended up struggling with for many years to come.

At twenty-two, I decided I would try talking to a therapist about it. It was something I hadn't done before and was hopeful it would help. During one of my first visits my therapist asked me to express how I felt, I'm sure to gauge the severity of the situation and to better help diagnose me. Words have never been easy for me and I had a hard time describing to him what it was that I was going through and how I had been feeling every day for years. One word kept coming to mind though, and somehow it felt like the perfect description of this seemingly never-ending internal struggle.

"I just feel... saggy." I told him. The word seemed to pique his interest. Knowing that I was studying illustration in school, he challenged me to draw this "saggy," feeling. At first I wasn't sure how I was going to fulfill this assignment. It felt so abstract and I struggled with finding the right images to accurately pinpoint my feelings.

Eventually, it came to me one day while in the shower as hot water rushed over my face. I pictured my mind as its own sort of town. Saggy Town. The idea interested me and it somehow felt cathartic to think of exploring my own mind through this town perspective. I decided that every day I would draw an element from or an aspect of this town whether it be food, cars, or characters. As part of this new project, I also decided to share my daily illustrations on Instagram.

After just two weeks I began to notice something. This town I was creating connected and resonated with people from all over the world. Comments were pouring in and the Saggy Town community began to grow. One hundred, then a thousand, then ten thousand people started to follow along on my journey, and it just kept climbing. In the height of my struggles, it had always felt like I was so alone. But throughout the process of sharing my artwork I was able to truly realize that it was not just me facing these monsters—it was everyone.

We are all fighting demons in our lives. We all have mountains to climb. We all know what that deep, dark, and lonely pit of despair feels like. This story isn't meant to be a self-help book or road map to guide you through the foggy darkness of life, but it is a reminder that this story is all of ours. Yes,

Juicebox is me. But he is also you, your mom, your dad, your friends, and neighbors. This is <u>all of our</u> story. I wanted you to know that the next time you feel overcome with darkness, when you feel so tired and ready to give up, when the stress and anxiety you face makes you feel like you can't bear it any longer, please remember this—you are not alone. Don't give up. Keep living. Keep trying. Things will get better.

- Caleb Staker

# Chapter 1

*"One need not be a chamber to be haunted."*
-Emily Dickinson

Amid a dark, musky, swamp-like bedroom littered with posters of rock bands, skateboarding, and the occasional 80's monster movie, lived a boy named Juicebox. Of course, his parents didn't intend for this to be his name. His mom had high hopes for a classic, biblical name to anoint her only son but she made the fatal error of giving him the initials of J.B. He was therefore destined to be referred to as such by his relatives and family friends, who were more than thrilled to knight him with the beloved nickname of these two distinguished consonants (much to his mother's chagrin.)

The title, Juicebox, came just a few years later when he entered his first years of school. *"What does J.B. stand for?"* his friends would ask. Our young hero, not ever being a fan of the combination of letters his mother scrawled across his birth certificate, chose for himself a much more exciting, much more enticing name as he swigged down his favorite beverage of cartoned fruit punch in the school cafeteria. "Juicebox, of course!"

The name had a certain *je ne sais quoi* and somehow stuck throughout the years, even with Mom and Dad. Juicebox always considered this the heist of the century, stealing away his old name and replacing it with his own creation.

It was this same stubborn independence that created this swamp that was his room. His small tv in the corner was surrounded by video game cartridges, unintentionally strewn into an exceptional model of the leaning Tower of Pisa, with tangled cords swirling in knotted rivers surrounding the structure. Piles of clothes, shoes, and last night's pizza covered all the other surfaces.

Most sane individuals would consider Juicebox's quarters to be completely unlivable. But Juicebox wasn't worried about cleanliness or organization. Like most kids, he had much grander things on his mind. Like the great zombie adventures, he'd read about in his comic books, or the detailed narratives of his favorite video games – and most of all, the many stories, poems and illustrations that he loved to pen throughout his notebooks.

If there was one thing Juicebox loved as much as the blue-haired, punk rock goddess that was Stacy Johnson, it was stories. Notebooks and sketch pads littered his room. Creative storytelling was second nature to him. Drawing the perfect illustration wasn't just a doodle and was certainly more important than whatever homework the notebooks were intended to be used for.

The power of a story was the common thread that connected the comics, video games, and notebooks in Juicebox's head and heart. That thread helped to hold him together. He used stories as an escape route, but they were also the medicine he needed to free his mind from the bonds of his emotions. Without the life of a story, his life was a never-ending existence of monotony and boredom.

It felt like nothing in his life ever changed. It was always the same tired cycle of school, chores, and high expectations — rinse and repeat. With always the hint of some unknown, unarticulated despair that seemed to manage to drain his mood down to the sewer of his sadness. Not that his life was all that bad. Juicebox and his parents lived in a mediocre house in a mediocre town. He always had food to eat, and his parents didn't fight every night. But even so, Juicebox struggled to find joy.

He couldn't decipher the exact moment he realized it – this lack of joy. It was as if he simply woke up one day and realized he hadn't felt truly happy in a long, long time. Perhaps it was the dyslexia, he thought, which made him feel isolated from the kids in his class – always being forced to come home and face the disappointment of his dad when he'd hand him yet another report card with a large red, "F" on the math and reading sections.

Or perhaps it was the anxiety that seemed to come over him for what felt like no reason at all during seemingly normal times of the day and night. Or it could be the intrusive thoughts that liked to run rampant within his mind. Sometimes these thoughts were full of fear, like the possibility of his parents getting divorced someday or that he would be held back a grade this year. But most of the time, they were simply there. Always rushing and running back and forth, like a stampede of fire ants stinging him with this memory, that idea, and this other issue. Never-ending, always swarming in his mind.

Whatever the cause, with every passing day, Juicebox was growing more and more agitated, lonely, and stressed with what felt like a dark haze beginning to cover his life. He wanted to run from it, but there was no escape. Except for sleep, of course. Wonderful, glorious sleep…

Beep, Beep, Beep! Juicebox smashed his fist down onto his alarm clock, executing a swift death to the cause of the annoying, unwanted sound that filled the crusty air. He rolled over as a warrior victorious to assume the most comfortable position within his grimy, pizza-stained sheets. It was just as the inklings of a snore began to resume its song, and the drool from his mouth pooled on the verge of falling down his chin when a remembrance struck his brain. "It's Saturday! Ah, haha!"

The clarion call of the weekend gave animation to his previously zombie-like body as if a sudden bolt of electricity zapped him up and out of his bed. He ran a rushed hand through his sun-streaked blonde hair and snatched up the closest available t-shirt to give it a quick sniff. Determining it to be somewhat acceptable, he began the hero's journey out of his room, dodging each pizza box and large pile of dirty clothes, while managing to only knock over one can of half-drunken soda. He grabbed the skateboard leaning up beside the door and made a conscious effort not to look back at the state of his living quarters before closing the door behind him.

The smell that greeted him upon evacuation was one of pure delight. Cinnamon pancakes, bacon, and fresh orange juice from the kitchen beckoned to him. He practically floated to his seat beside Dad at the kitchen table and swiftly began to shove crispy pieces of bacon into his mouth and drizzle Mom's homemade strawberry syrup all over his pancakes.

"Your cooking is pure magic, mom. Did you make a deal with a witch to teach you how to make these pancakes? Did you sell your firstborn? Do I have a secret older brother living with Rumpelstiltskin or something? Because if so I wouldn't blame you." He stuffed a fork full of pancakes into his mouth. "This food was worth however many firstborns you had to give up."

His mother laughed and looked up from her many pans on the stove, flashing Juicebox a smile. Juicebox always loved his mother's smile. It was big and bright and welcoming, and always seemed to paint a sparkle into her deep hazel eyes. "No firstborns." She started scrubbing some dishes from behind the counter. "It was just a small fairy gift given to me upon my birth." Juicebox gulped down his juice in one swift chug, a slight smile splaying on his mouth. Mom always played along with his fairytale antics. "That makes *so* much sense," he gasped with a newly clad orange mustache. Mom winked at him. "I'm glad you like it."

Dad was reading the newspaper in his usual position, long thin legs crossed at the other end of the table, with his oak-colored hair hanging slightly in his eyes as he read. He reached for a piece of bacon as he continued to read but his fingers came back simply covered with only the grease left on the empty bacon plate. He sighed tiredly, as was his custom, and peeked over the top of his newspaper.

"Hey Juicebox, did you get that homework done?" He took a handkerchief from his pocket and wiped the grease from his hand. "You know, the weekends are perfect for getting ahead." Juicebox rolled his eyes and looked down at his plate, shaking his head. All previous feelings of rest and whimsy being flushed from his body like water down a toilet.

He sighed, attempting to hold in his annoyance. "Why do you always want my life to suck so much, Dad?" He pushed his plate to the side, suddenly not feeling so hungry anymore. "I go to school every day of the week and Saturdays are the one day I can escape that soul crushing building and my nasty toad of a teacher, Mrs. Gill."

Juicebox could almost see the steam slowly beginning to puff from his dad's ears, which were already taking on a pinkish hue. Dad leaned in a little closer, arching an eyebrow. "You should talk nicer about your teachers, son." He shook his newspaper back into place and resumed his morning reading. Juicebox laughed and pinched the bridge of his nose in frustration. "That old hag is evil, dad!" Mom lifted a wooden spoon from the sink and shook it disapprovingly. "Be nice, Juicebox. We raised you better than that." Juicebox rolled his eyes again. "Did you know that she took a ruler to Stacy's hand last week for passing a note?! A note, mom! Stacy still has welts from it. I thought that corporal punishment was illegal in schools now!"

Mom's eyes widened as she lifted her yellow rubber gloved hand to her mouth in shock, the rubber squeaking from the twist of her wrist. "Oh, that is terrible!" Dad glanced back at mom and then turned to face Juicebox again. "Your mother is right. That isn't okay. Frankly, it's a little alarming... But Stacy should know better than to be disruptive in class like that…" He shook his head. "I worry about those friends of yours. You need to be careful with who you let influence you."

Juicebox covered his face with both hands and tried to hide the pure annoyance he felt making its way to his expression. Dad glanced back at mom again. "We should probably look into that whole ruler incident a little more though..." Mom nodded in agreement.

Juicebox massaged his temples, doing his best to summon all the willpower he contained to remain calm. "Yeah, well... That's a big no on the homework for me." He chugged down another large glass of orange juice and shuddered as he slammed the glass back down onto the table, his eyes wandering to the ceiling. "Ugh, just the thought of school stresses me out."

Mom's brows arched in concern as she began layering pans into the dishwasher. "I thought you liked art class?" Juicebox remained silent. Dad set his newspaper down on the table and adjusted himself in his seat. "Well, you're not the only one stressed out. I've got a whole bunch of stuff to do for work today." Mom heaved out an irritated sigh. Dad continued,

"And I'm not going to get much of it done because we have to go to your mom's cousin's wedding." Mom, who visibly did not appreciate this comment from dad, forced a smile. "Don't forget Juicebox, you're coming too."

This was the final blow, the guillotine blade blazing down upon his weekend. Juicebox immediately threw up his arms, shaking his head vigorously. "Ah Mom! This is my one day. Stacy and Jefferson are waiting to go skate with me as we speak!" Mom nodded. "You can go out skateboarding with your friends. Just be home by eleven so we can leave for the wedding."

Juicebox snatched a spare pancake from the table and stood up with his skateboard to exit the house through the side kitchen door. "You don't know how much this sucks!" All efforts at remaining calm vanished from his body as he slammed the door behind him. Dad wiped his hand across his face in annoyance, shaking his head with frustration. "Want me to go after him?" Mom quietly filled the dishwasher with soap and shook her head. "No. Let him have his time. We'll talk about the attitude later tonight." She looked out the kitchen window. Something was deeply wrong. She felt a strange prickling rush up the back of her neck and thrum anxiously through her heart but couldn't quite place its origin.

# Chapter 2

*"Now let it work. Mischief, thou art afoot. Take thou what course thou wilt."*
-William Shakespeare

"Why do they always have to do this to me?" Juicebox muttered. As much as Juicebox would be happy never leaving his bedroom, he wouldn't spend his Saturday morning doing homework until it was time to head off to some distant cousin's wedding. Saturdays were supposed to be his, the one day to do what he needed to keep him going for the rest of the week—and what he needed was waiting for him at the skatepark, his best friends.

Stacy Johnson and Jefferson Richards were the constant supporters who grounded Juicebox to the real world. When he was with them, he could almost forget his hidden sadness. The three of them had been best friends since grade school. Stacy and Jefferson were there when he officially transformed into Juicebox all those years ago in the school cafeteria. The childhood they spent together was the closest thing Juicebox had to golden pirate treasure. He wouldn't trade them, or the bond they shared for anything in the world.

Juicebox was walking on automatic. His body instinctively knew where to go. Yet, even walking on autopilot, he still noticed the run-down look of his neighborhood. There were cracks all up and down the sidewalks and streets, overgrown grass, and crooked power lines that appeared to go in all directions. Dad was always complaining about the lack of curb appeal, making repair calls to the city that never seemed to go through. Juicebox didn't mind. Honestly, he thought it was more fun this way. The grim look of what was once a lovely, well-to-do suburb beginning to crumble resonated within him and inspired the scenery of many of the odd adventures he enjoyed writing.

This was a place that made sense. Sure, it used to be brand new, with fresh white paint on the houses, and butterfly gardens in the yards. But things don't stay brand new forever. White paint eventually begins to flake away, and rain and windstorms always come and drown out the flowers. People shouldn't expect perfection. Not when life demanded to be lived. Not when problems insisted on reoccurring.

What he did mind was what his mom felt. She was always saying things like, *"I just wish we were able to get the house we wanted."* Or *"This neighborhood sure didn't turn out the way we hoped."* It never seemed like she was happy with where she was at. Her lack of satisfaction was palpable, and it made Juicebox feel sad. A kind of sadness he couldn't quite figure out. When she said things like this, it made him feel like he needed to pick her a flower from the garden or bring her breakfast in bed. It was like she was saying that this life they lived together just wasn't good enough, that she didn't get the life that she had always hoped for.

These thoughts often followed Juicebox as he walked down these streets. He tried shooing them away today, instead trying to focus on a game of I-spy hoping to find some weird new junk in his neighbors' yards to inspect later – but as he walked, the thoughts inside his mind seemed to grow stronger. His shoulders felt heavy and with each step, his thoughts grew louder and louder until suddenly, he heard an actual voice.

*"USELESS..."*

Juicebox stopped and looked around but couldn't see anybody there. It spoke again, in a whisper, *"USELESS, WORTHLESS, WASTE OF SPACE! IDIOT! NOBODY LIKES YOU!"* Juicebox was startled and spun around quickly to see who it was. But again, there was nobody there…

Anxiously, Juicebox picked up his pace, continuously looking over his shoulder. The voices started again. *"OF COURSE, YOUR MOTHER IS UNHAPPY. SHE HAS YOU FOR A SON."* The voice laughed. *"YOU DRIVE YOUR DAD CRAZY BECAUSE YOU JUST AREN'T SMART. IT'S NO WONDER WHY YOU DO SO BADLY IN SCHOOL. YOU AREN'T CAPABLE OF DOING WELL."*

Now the voice was a scream as if someone was standing just behind him. His heart felt as if it had plummeted into his stomach and the air was sucked from his lungs. The primal instinct to run sent Juicebox darting across the street. He needed to get away from the voice. It was like nails scraping down a chalkboard. Two steps into the road and Juicebox's foot landed in a puddle of strange purple ooze. The sticky hold of the goo tugged back on his foot, interrupting his run.

"What the–"

He pulled hard to free himself, but the ooze seemed to have a death grip hold on his foot. An evil laugh rattled in his brain.

*"I'M COMING FOR YOU."*

The roaring sound of a horn from an obnoxious and impatient driver blared loudly at him. The rude honk snapped Juicebox's attention back to reality. The driver looked annoyed.

"Hey, kid! Watch where you're going! This is a street!"

Juicebox glanced at his foot. The ooze was gone. But his foot felt like ice. He shook himself from the eeriness he felt, chalking it up to his wild imagination and skated off into town to find his friends.

◻ ◻ ◻

If there was one place in the world that felt like a refuge from Juicebox's life, other than his bedroom, it was the skate park. Unlike most parts of the cement-laden town, the skate park was green. Tall, thick pine trees stretched high and wide, creating a cool and shady fortress surrounding the skating area. A creek hid just a few yards back, which was perfect for soaking your feet after a long day of skating — and hot dog Steve always posted his cart just up the street so there was always a delicious snack nearby. Whatever he heard or saw a few moments prior couldn't get him as long as he was here, safe in his fortress.

Jefferson saw Juicebox skating towards him and quickly rubbed at the lenses of his thick glasses with his sweatshirt to make sure he was seeing properly. He thought Juicebox looked a little off, like he was being chased by zombies or something. His face was pale, and he raced to where Jefferson stood as if his life depended on it. The urgency of his run and the fear splayed on Juicebox's face sent shivers all over Jefferson's chocolate colored skin.

Always on the lookout for bully attacks, Jefferson instinctively looked past Juicebox to see who was chasing him. Bullies didn't bother them much now in high school, but after years of past abuse, the instinct to run was an automatic response for Jefferson. Juicebox nearly fell off his board when he finally reached him.

"Juicebox! Who's after you, man?" Jefferson asked, still surveying the perimeter of the skate park.

"No one. I don't know. Something really weird just happened, but I'm pretty sure it was just my imagination," Juicebox said.

Juicebox knew the ooze disappeared, but the coldness of its touch still crawled up his leg and showed on his face. His eyes were wide as he thought about the voice that had taunted him. They darted around the park, searching for more potential weirdness until they landed on Stacy.

She skated up beside Jefferson and took off her helmet. Instantly, all Juicebox could focus on were the waves of blue hair bouncing in the sunlight creating a soft ocean glow around her head that reflected off of her black leather jacket. Stacy's hair always made her eyes stand out. Juicebox loved those big bright eyes, and his frightened face softened when those eyes met his.

"Juicebox! Really, are you good? What did you see?" Jefferson insisted and slapped a hand on his friend's back. Stacy didn't have the same effect on Jefferson, and he was still looking for a possible enemy attack coming from behind Juicebox.

"What?" Juicebox mumbled, still entranced.

"What do you mean what?" Jefferson waved a hand in front of Juicebox's face in an attempt to bring his friend back to reality. Stacy laughed heartily and flipped her hair back. "He just gets starstruck in my presence, that's all." At this statement of the painfully obvious, Juicebox felt the fear of many young teen boys when they realize that their cheeks have turned bright pink and did the only thing that made sense to his mind in the moment, which was to shove her as if he were still ten years old. "Shut up!" He laughed playfully, attempting to ward off his embarrassment.

Stacy stumbled backward and gave him a face of surprise and hurt. The blood which pinked his cheeks just moments before now flooded his face completely as his eyes immediately widened in horror, reaching out toward her. "Jeez, Stacy, I'm sorry, I didn't mean–" Stacy laughed, and shoved him

back. Juicebox stumbled backward and chuckled as he shoved her again. Jefferson rolled his eyes. "Are you two just going to stand around and flirt all day, or are we going to have some fun?" In unison, Juicebox and Stacy both turned toward Jefferson with semi-embarrassed expressions. Juicebox, who by then was just about as red as a cherry on a hot summer day, hesitated and glanced nervously at Stacy.

Stacy glanced back at him, arching her eyebrows menacingly. "On the count of three…. One, two, three!" She yelled as they both gave Jefferson a large shove. "Hey!" Jefferson cried out, laughing. "I'm not affiliated with your weird banter!"

Juicebox laughed and shook his head giving Jefferson a final shove before grabbing his board and puffing out his chest to announce his idea for their weekend plans. "As our beloved leader, I say that we do something extra adventurous today."

Jefferson scoffed. "Our leader?"

Stacy interjected "If anyone's the leader, we all know it's me."

Juicebox arched an eyebrow mischievously. "Do you guys want to hear my idea or not?" The two others crossed their arms. Juicebox rolled his eyes and continued on.

"So, this morning my dad thought it would be a good idea to do some homework today…"

Stacy and Jefferson's faces flooded with disgust.

"Wait a second... You're not actually suggesting we do homework on a Saturday are you?" Stacy made a noise reminiscent of gagging.

Juicebox let out a little laugh.

"Stacy, please. Do you not know me?"

Stacy smiled. "Well then, keep going! Don't make us wait! What is it?"

Juicebox cleared his throat before continuing. "Well... The homework thing got me thinking. We all know that Mrs. Gill is expecting detailed projects about amphibians from each of us early Monday morning, right?"

Stacy and Jefferson nodded their heads. Juicebox nonchalantly shoved a hand inside his pocket, with a hint of trickery pulling slyly at the corner of his mouth.

"Well... I say we give her a froggy project she'll never forget."

His friends remained silent, each appearing to work out this riddle in their own minds. They knew how much he loved them pulling ideas out of him. Jefferson laughed "Dude what the heck is that supposed to mean?"

Juicebox held up a finger and closed his eyes. "Listen. What do you hear?"

Stacy looked over in the direction of the creek hidden by a grove of trees.

"Frogs." A smile started to form on her face.

"Oh, no," Jefferson said, with a roll of his eyes.

All of the humor went out of Juicebox's voice as his tone turned menacing.

"After what that witch did to Stacy last week? Oh yes." Stacy looked down at her hand, where an angry red mark still crossed the tops of her knuckles.

"I'm in," said Stacy. "What are you planning?"

Juicebox grinned mischievously. "We need to gather a few frogs for our beloved teacher so she can see how seriously we take her assignments. We take our captured frogs to the school and stuff them into her desk. I can't wait to see her joy on Monday morning when she has drawers overflowing with frogs to share with the class."

"Juicebox, your sincerity is just too much," Stacy smiled as her eyes glazed over, imagining the hectic scene.

Jefferson pinched at the bridge of his nose, then glanced at Stacy's hand once more. He took a deep breath. "Okay. Let's do it."

¤¤¤

Jefferson and Juicebox had dug a few old grocery bags out of a nearby garbage can to hold their captured frogs, and the three friends walked into the cool waters of the park creek with rolled up pant legs and excited, nervous jitters. The little green friends they heard ribbiting just moments before went silent as they entered the water.

"How are we going to find these things?" Asked Jefferson.

"SHHH," snapped Stacy. "Open your eyes and look around."

"I see one!" He whispered back.

Within a half hour, Jefferson and Stacy had several frogs squirming in their bags. Juicebox on the other hand, seemed to catch nothing but mud, which covered him nearly head to toe.

"Juice, if you try taking a step into the creek without creating a mini tsunami you might have more success." Stacy winked at him. Jefferson snickered.

"Dude for real, you're trying to catch frogs, not recreate a Godzilla scene." His friends laughed until they found it hard to breathe. Juicebox rolled his eyes, thanking his lucky stars that his newly reddened cheeks were hidden by a thick coat of mud. Determined, he dove for the next flash of green that caught the corner of his eye. He came up for air holding the biggest, ugliest frog he had ever seen. It immediately made a strong wriggle toward freedom.

"Guys help!" he shouted. "I caught the biggest frog in the creek!"

Jefferson burst out laughing again. "Maybe you should actually do this week's reading on amphibians. That's not a frog. You just caught the perfect toad for your school project."

Stacy clapped for his toady success. Even though she did it primly with the mocking air of a fancy Victorian woman in a ballgown, Juicebox still marked it down as a win.

"Here, drop him into this bag before he gets away," she said.

And then they were off, each teen tightly gripping a squirming bag of amphibians as they skated toward the high school.

At the edge of the school property, they scoped out the building and surrounding parking lot to see if a Saturday activity brought students back to school on the weekend. The school looked deserted. Juicebox smiled thankfully and breathed a sigh of relief.

He smoothly motioned for his friends to follow him as they made their way toward their classroom window, noticing that it was cracked open ever so slightly.

Jefferson looked at Juicebox suspiciously. "You had this planned, didn't you?"

"Maybe. Let's just say no one, not even a teacher, can hurt my friends and get away with it."

"My hero." Stacy said in a tone that Juicebox couldn't decipher. "Let's just hurry and get out of here."

Juicebox turned to Jefferson. "Here, hold this bag while I get in."

Juicebox balanced one foot on his skateboard and the other on a brick that jutted out from the wall to push the window open a bit more and jumped quickly through the narrow opening. Stacy and Jefferson cringed as a loud clanging of what seemed to be Juicebox knocking over a desk and chairs during his landing rang in their ears. They looked at each other with painful expressions. A moment later Juicebox popped his head out of the window with a clumsy smile.

"Discreet as always, Mr. Bond." Stacy teased.

"Just hand me the bags," Juicebox said, rolling his eyes as Jefferson chuckled. Securing the goods, he retreated back into the classroom.

Juicebox made quick business of stuffing the frogs into the drawers of Mrs. Gill's desk, saving the giant toad for the top drawer as if it were the cherry on top of a revenge-filled sundae. As he stuffed the drawers like stockings on Christmas morning, he noticed a purple tar-like slime dripping from the corner of the desk onto the floor.

"This school is disgusting," he shuddered, as his mind drifted to the recent memory of the similar looking gunk that he had stepped in that morning. He peered at it more closely for a moment and the room fell silent. All croaks coming from the desk drawers faded away and the light from the window in the classroom seemed to dim.

*"WORTHLESS LOSER..."*

He spun around, but the classroom was empty. The spark of mischievous fun that he felt mere moments before was snuffed out like a candle in the night. He needed to leave this room now. And that need bubbled up in his throat like nervous stomach acid. He knew something was messing with him. Something *was* following him. Juicebox didn't care about frogs or teachers anymore. He wanted to be out in the sun with his skateboard and his friends. He needed to run away from the darkness that was closing in.

He made an eager leap through the window and it felt like breaching through a veil that separated the dark from the light. The sunshine hit his skin and the normal noises of the day returned to his ears as he heard Jefferson and Stacy joking with each other, waiting for Juicebox to finish up with his froggy business. They didn't seem to feel the darkness like he did.

He hit the ground with a thud, ripping a hole through his already holey jeans — but the pain from the fall felt like a welcome kiss compared to the darkness he just experienced in the classroom. With all the rebel confidence he went into the school with now gone, he glanced up at the window expecting to see a demon leering back at him.

Stacy rushed to his side, placing her hand on his shoulder. She worried someone was in the classroom and their prank was discovered. Her touch did its magic and brought him back to the moment.

He looked into her eyes to ground himself and let out a half-hearted chuckle to shake off the last of the creeping dread he had felt inside the classroom.

"That was wild," he said. "I can't wait to see the circus of frogs explode from Mrs. Gill's desk on Monday…"

"You look like you saw a ghost in there. Everything okay?" Jefferson asked.

Juicebox tried not to hesitate in his answer, "Everything's great. Frogs and toads are hiding in the desk, all ready to go." He stood up and shook himself off. "Let's get out of here. The last one to the park is a Mrs. Gill!"

# Chapter 3

*"It cannot be seen, cannot be felt,*
*Cannot be heard, cannot be smelt,*
*It lies behind stars and under hills,*
*And empty holes it fills,*
*It comes first and follows after*
*Ends life, kills laughter."*
-J.R.R. Tolkien

Juicebox felt like he could fly once the wheels of his skateboard hit the pavement. The wind from his speed nearly blew his hat from his head as the three friends raced in tandem, each trying to overtake the other and move their racing position to first place. As they crossed the street where the park entrance lay, an orange station wagon intercepted their perfect escape into the park. The tires screeched as the car stopped right in front of the gang of friends.

They slammed their feet to the ground to stop themselves from hitting the vehicle that suddenly blocked their path. The color from Juicebox's face drained as realization hit him.

"I totally forgot!" he blurted.

Stacy gave Juicebox a concerned look.

"What is it? What's going on?"

Juicebox's dad rolled down the car window with a glint of fury in his eyes, and angry words hiding badly behind his clenched teeth.

"Get in the car, Juicebox." He tried to sound calm, but hiding his emotions was never Dad's strong suit.

Juicebox rolled his eyes and briefly considered his next move.

"Get in the car… NOW!"

Juicebox turned to his friends. "I gotta go. I'll try to catch up with you guys later today." He looked down at the ground and sheepishly walked to the car, opened the door, then slammed it closed in a huff. Without a pause, the tires screeched again as the car sped off in the opposite direction of the skate park.

Juicebox looked out the back window and saw Stacy and Jefferson left in a cloud of dust, growing smaller and smaller as the station wagon raced away. He settled into his seat; arms crossed in an angry pout. His dad broke the awkward silence with a cutting tone that shot toward Juicebox like a dagger.

"Do you know what time it is?"

"Come on, Dad. You know I don't have a watch."

"Do you remember that your mother asked you to be home in time to go to the wedding?"

"Vaguely." Juicebox looked out the window and tried to think about being anywhere else but the back of this car getting lectured at by his dad for the one-millionth time.

Dad's eyes snapped toward Juicebox from the rearview mirror. "Do you think you could have tried to watch the time just once in your life? When are you going to learn a little responsibility?" Dad's eyebrows were laced with frustration.

"You could have gone without me. I hate these family things. Why would I want to go to some stupid wedding when I could be doing something fun on the

ONE day I have free?" He lowered his voice to a mumble. "It's not like any of this matters to me."

"Juicebox!" His mom scowled as she turned to meet his face. He saw the hurt in her eyes, but he was beyond worrying about what she felt right now.

"I never have any time to do what I want! And you act so surprised when I don't want to be around you when I'm home!" he raged without censure. "Maybe I wouldn't be so miserable if you would just listen to me sometimes. You never listen to me! I don't believe you even care about me!"

"Juicebox, of course we care about you! I'm really sorry you don't want to go to the wedding but it's for the family," his mom wiped away a tear. "It's going to mean a lot to your cousin that you're there."

Her voice was growing smaller and sadder with each word.

"My cousin... " Juicebox laughed sarcastically. "She doesn't even know my name."

"Well, it means a lot to your dad and me that you are with us," his mom added.

"Yeah, right." Juicebox scoffed.

His dad looked away from the road and glared at Juicebox from the mirror.

"You really know how to push buttons, young man."

Juicebox locked his eyes with his dad's angry gaze. "And you really know how to suck, old man." Juicebox mumbled beneath his breath.

Juicebox's mom tried to mute her crying while Dad reached over to comfort her with a hand on her shoulder. He steered the car to the on-ramp of the highway as it filled with an uncomfortable silence. Mom turned back toward Juicebox.

"Your clothes are in that bag. You can change in the car when we get there."

"Whatever," Juicebox sighed as he rolled his eyes.

Whatever small semblance of patience Dad had been trying to grasp onto burst free in an instant.

"Don't you dare talk to your mom that way! Apologize!"

Juicebox glared back at his dad, refusing to comply.

"Juicebox, I mean it!" His dad looked away from the road again and stared back at Juicebox through the mirror, their eyes locked and loaded, like an old western standoff.

Juicebox knew he was being a jerk. He was just too far into his annoyance now, anger blurring all his sensitivities.

"Juicebox. I SAID—!"

A horn blared.

Everyone turned their attention to the traffic in front of them, but the reaction came too late. Within seconds, the orange station wagon crossed the middle lane of the road and raced at high speed into the oncoming traffic on the other side. There was a scraping of metal, a crunching of debris, and the sound of his mother's scream as the world around Juicebox slowly faded away.

¤¤¤

Juicebox felt himself being pulled from a dark hole as he shook his head. His ears rang, and everything sounded fuzzy, buzzing, and far away. He put his hand instinctively to his nose and felt the foreign sensation of sticky wet blood running down his face. He looked up, not sure where he was, then saw his parents slumped over in the front seat of the car.

The wedding.

The argument.

"Mo…Mom? Dad?"

Juicebox was aware of people screaming and sirens blaring from all directions. The frantic movements of unknown people outside the car did not pop the dazed bubble that Juicebox was trapped in. Uncontrolled tears started to blur his vision as the bubble burst, and the outside chaos flooded into the car as a fireman reached in towards him.

"Son, can you hear me? Do you feel any specific pain anywhere? We're going to get you out of this car," he cut away at the seatbelt that was strapping Juicebox to the scraps of metal surrounding him.

"I...I..." He started to say. "Mom..." Juicebox wanted his parents to wake up and look back at him. He needed them to look at him and tell him that everything would be okay.

The fireman was moving Juicebox out from the car door as panic exploded inside him. He had to save his parents.

"Mom! Dad!" He shouted as he wrestled to get away from the fireman and rush back to his parents. The further he moved from the accident scene, the better he could take in the entire view of the smashed car. The front end of the car was destroyed, a tangled mess of metal that no one could have survived. Why was he still here?

Juicebox screamed as he looked back at the car, still lunging and pulling away from the hands of the fireman. He sucked in smoke-filled air, the gassy fumes giving him a dizzy buzz. No matter how hard he fought, he lost the battle against the muscles holding him back. Juicebox was quickly rushed into an ambulance, then given a drug that silenced his shock and screams. The slumped-over image of his parents in the mangled front seat of the family car was the last thing he saw before everything went black again.

¤¤¤

A scream woke Juicebox from his drug-induced sleep. Confused, his eyes raced around the dark room he found himself in — shock penetrating his core as he realized it was his own scream coming from deep inside where a voice repeated in low disturbing gargles, *"IT'S ALL YOUR FAULT! IT'S ALL YOUR FAULT! IT'S ALL YOUR FAULT!"*

"Stop!" he screamed out loud. "I can't take it anymore!" A panic attack was about to vomit out of him like a volcanic eruption. If there were an explosion, it would suck the air out of his existence. He needed someone to talk to him now. Where were his parents? Where were Stacy and Jefferson? What happened? This was more than a nightmare.

*"IT'S ALL YOUR FAULT! IT'S ALL YOUR FAULT! IT'S ALL YOUR FAULT!"* The voice never went away.

A nurse suddenly walked into his room. She looked back at another nurse and a doctor who were standing in front of the hospital room's door. In the flash moment of seeing them, Juicebox knew they had been talking about him. He felt like the world must be talking about him, and the weight of that world crushed him.

Hospital machines beeped in chorus with the dark voice inside his mind. Juicebox looked down at his arm, where tubes were attached to him like tentacles securing themselves to a machine that towered above him. The beeping meant he must be alive, and that this was really happening.

Reality crashed upon him like a cold wave. He focused all of his energy on the singular hope that somewhere in this hospital was a room where his parents lay on beds like his, listening to the same beeping noises that filled his ears. They were alive and worried about him. Wondering where he was. Demanding that the doctors take them to him. A creeping dread dragged that hope out of his mind.

"I can't breathe," he croaked. He wanted to say that something was trying to kill him, but all he could do was look around in panic.

"Do you know where you are?" the nurse asked him as she handed him a cup of water. "Take some small sips of this."

"I'm in a hospital!" Juicebox's voice came out tense and biting. "Where the hell is the doctor? I need to know my parents are okay." The nurse kept shining a light in his eyes and jotting down quick notes in a small pad of paper that she held in her hand. She looked at him but said nothing.

Seconds later, the door opened with the same doctor Juicebox had seen in the hall. He came to the bed where Juicebox was sitting, followed by a police officer. Both men looked grim. Juicebox didn't want to be here in this moment. He didn't belong in this moment. This moment was saved for nightmares and sad movies that he avoided at all costs. His head started to swim again. His chest felt like a giant fist was squeezing all the air from his lungs. The panic was intense now. Juicebox gasped for breath.

*"IT'S ALL YOUR FAULT!"*

He looked at the doctor without really seeing him. "I need my mom and dad now!" His voice was an intense whisper, cracking as his body shook.

"Juicebox, I'm Doctor Zobell. I want you to just take some slow, deep breaths." The doctor started to breathe in slowly and deeply, hoping this example would trigger Juicebox to follow his lead. "Come on and breathe with me. Amazingly, you don't have any serious injuries. But you will probably feel a little beat up for a while."

Juicebox attempted to breathe but was only able to manage a jagged gasp as he swam through waves of complete panic. His ears rang, drowning out everything the doctor said to him.

"Listen, kid. I'm sorry you have to be here and I'm sorry we have to do this now," the officer said. "Is there anyone you can call? A family member, maybe, who lives in the area?"

"I need my mom and dad."

The nurse reached out and took Juicebox's hand while the doctor stepped in a little closer and put his hand on Juicebox's shoulder.

Time stopped.

The ringing in his ears stopped.

His breathing stopped.

The world felt like it stood frozen in that moment. If he never heard what needed to be said, there would be hope that life would go back to the way it was that morning. Mom's pancakes. Dad's newspaper. His bedroom swamp waiting for his return. His *life*.

"Juicebox, I'm sorry," the doctor started. Juicebox stopped listening before the doctor could say what he already knew, "Your parents didn't make it." The second hand clicked now on the other side of that frozen moment and moved Juicebox one tick away from the last morning he spent with his parents. The clock was merciless and pushed him forward. His heart snapped as the cup of water he held in his hand just moments before splashed on the floor along with tears that finally broke free from the dam of his denial. He curled himself into a ball on the bed and cried, feeling completely and utterly alone in this world with nobody but the sickly, mocking whisper coming from some dark corner of his brain.

"THIS WAS ALL YOUR FAULT."

*THIS WAS ALL YOUR FAULT.
THIS WAS ALL YOUR FAULT."*

# CHAPTER 4

*"Deep in earth my love is lying
And I must weep alone."*
-Edgar Allen Poe

Juicebox attended the memorial service for his parents in a daze. He shook hands with people he had never seen before. People told him how great his parents were. People offered to help him with anything he might need. He stood next to the closed caskets and tried to remember what his parents looked like. Their faces changed in his mind like characters making faces for a camera. One minute they were smiling at him, then he vividly saw their angry expressions, just like the ones he invoked during the frequent fights he had instigated with them lately. He tried to block out those angry expressions only to hear the all too familiar whisper that had followed him everywhere since the accident.

*"THIS WAS YOUR FAULT. AND EVERYONE KNOWS IT."*

He wondered now if it was his fault. He wasn't the one driving. Juicebox could feel angry at his dad for being the one behind the wheel. Anger diverted his guilt from drowning him completely. So much anger. Before the accident his mom was angry with him sometimes. His dad seemed angry at him all of the time. Juicebox fought back by being angry as well. Now, he was just angry that his parents left him behind.

The anger didn't stick around. It was too exhausting. So, other emotions started to take its place. Like smoke coming into a room from underneath the door, the pain of failure and loneliness seeped into Juicebox's head and heart. This smoke clouded his mind, making him feel like he was moving through his life in a darkened haze.

He didn't realize when the church funeral service ended and the graveside service started. Even though he survived the car crash that killed his parents, he was dead inside. The same people who shook his hand at the beginning of the funeral filed by him again, expressing their final words of grief and support. Stacy and Jefferson stood in the back of the crowd. They made their way to Juicebox as the crowd thinned out. They all three stood together in a group hug. Juicebox pulled his friends close and buried his face in their shoulders.

"I feel nothing," he whispered. "I think you guys should leave me alone for a while."

"It's okay," Jefferson squeezed his shoulder, concern filling his face for his friend.

"We're here when you need us," added Stacy. She looked at Jefferson and saw her own worry reflected in his eyes as well.

Juicebox didn't respond. He couldn't look at his friends. His face was unreadable. A blank piece of paper with no desire to be written upon. He turned to face the newly dug graves of his parents, hearing and feeling nothing from the reality around him. Stacy and Jefferson watched him wipe at the flow of tears that streamed down his face. Stacy reached out to grab Jefferson's hand. He squeezed it in response.

Everyone left the gravesite eventually. There were no words they could say or acts of service they could do to change anything now. So, they left. As all funeral attendees eventually do. Leaving the grieving to the ones whose turn it was to go through hell. Juicebox stood motionless in the same place where Jefferson and Stacy left him. He was alone now. Left to stare forever into the inferno that was his reality. Nobody to blame but himself for the ferry ride over.

A small blue car raced to the curb a few yards away and honked several times. Juicebox ignored the sound and silently prayed that he could melt onto the ground and drain into the storm grate next to the grass. The horn insisted he pay attention when it sounded long and loud.

Juicebox angrily tore his eyes away from the graves. He recognized the car. It was more like a bucket of bolts held together with rust and luck. When the engine was running, doorknobs and radio dials shook so hard they threatened to fall apart completely. His mom hated riding in that car.

The window rolled down and the shriveled face of his grandma peered out from behind a pair of thick-lensed glasses.

He didn't see his grandma much when he was growing up. She was odd, even a little scary. Juicebox had a theory that she had killed his grandfather. But he could never prove it. She leaned out the window. A cigarette bounced and balanced between her lips, threatening to fall to the ground.

"Juicebox, the funeral is over; everyone's gone. It's time to go. You're with me now, kid," she called out.

Juicebox reluctantly slid into the passenger seat and looked out the window, not wanting to be in the car or even in his life. But what should he expect? Being in hell meant being tortured. There was no use in fighting against the stripes from Hades. He felt as if the world had stopped, and he didn't care if a semi-truck came and flattened him to the ground. *"Play stupid games, win stupid prizes."* His dad used to say. Juicebox knew deep down that was all he'd be getting out of this painful existence from here on out. Stupid prize after stupid prize.

He pulled his attention from the passing houses out the window to watch the circus act that his Grandma was exhibiting. She finished the cigarette dangling from her mouth and hurled it into the overflowing ashtray under the radio dials of the car, then dove her hand into her jacket pocket and fished around the loose potato sack dress that barely kept her from flashing every innocent bystander that whizzed by.

She finally found her buried treasure and moved a knobby knee to steady the steering wheel as she lit the fresh cigarette in one hand, with the lighter in the other. Her hands were shaking so violently that Juicebox couldn't help but feel slightly impressed when she finally got the lighter to hit the mark of the end of the cigarette. The car rattled and swerved the entire time. Juicebox was convinced he, too, would soon be dying in a car accident before the grass started to grow on his parent's graves.

"These things are going to kill me one day," Grandma said to herself.

Yes, thought Juicebox. A car crash certainly would kill both of them. And that was just fine with him.

"But I like them too much to quit. You don't mind if I smoke, do you, kid?" She asked. It was the first thing she had said directly to him since he got in the car. He didn't answer her. His grandma didn't seem to notice his silence.

"I have a room ready for you. I picked up a few things from your house. They're on the seat." Grandma's sentence echoed his mother's last words about clothes waiting on the seat for him and he felt a sudden jab to the heart. He wondered where that bag went after the crash and what his mom had picked out for him to wear to the wedding. An image of her carefully washing and ironing a dress shirt for him played in his mind and he was suddenly overcome with the desire to never wear clean clothes again.

"We can go back to your house and get some of your old things gathered in the next few days. But for now, at least you have a bed to sleep in."

The car bumped over every pothole in the road and swerved around imaginary obstacles, finally coming to a rough stop in front of a dilapidated old house that looked like it would crumble at the slightest gust of wind. Juicebox couldn't remember when he had last visited his grandmother's house.

The place was way creepier than he remembered. *They both could use a facelift,* he thought to himself.

"Home, Sweet Home," he said under his breath. The house needed paint and roof repairs. The yard was an overgrown mess of weeds, and rusty junk was strewn everywhere, hiding in the tall, dried lawn. Grandma fumbled with her keys until she found the one that opened the front door. It squeaked with a warning as it slowly cracked open.

"Your room is the first one down the hall. It used to be your mom's. Hope that's okay," she said as they stepped through the door. "I've been using the room mostly for storage. But the bed is still in there, along with an old TV." She looked at Juicebox and watched for some sign of life from him. He said nothing.

"Well, we'll get you set up soon." She hurried down the hall and Juicebox heard the bathroom door close. He stood alone in the entryway. A wave of exhaustion caused a slumping of his shoulders as he walked down the hall to his new room. He just wanted to be in his swamp where he could safely hide from the world. Nothing was familiar in this room.

No video games or posters, or pizza boxes, just an old mattress on top of a brass bed frame. Old, withered storage boxes cluttered the floor of the room.

"I know it's a mess," Grandma said from behind him. Juicebox jumped. How did she sneak up so silently? Maybe a car crash didn't kill him, but he wasn't so sure his grandma wouldn't.

"I'll get you some bedding while you get settled in," she said as she hobbled down the hall once more.

Juicebox dropped his skateboard and suitcase and then folded himself up on the bed. Tears began to flow without restraint.

"I am so alone," he sobbed to the wall. "I'm so depressed. How can I keep going? What's the point?" Familiar anger welled up from deep inside his soul.

He was angry at his parents, at the car that took away

his family, and at the world. Most of all he was angry at himself.

*"ALL YOUR FAULT, YOU PATHETIC LOSER."* He could never escape the whisper that left him feeling so empty.

His door creaked open again.

"Hey, kid, I brought you some cocoa. You like cocoa, right?" No answer. "We're still doing the silence thing. Okay, I get it." The sound of a dropped mug crashing to the floor echoed down the hall.

"Agh! I'll get you another one and maybe clean up that mess." Grandma's slippers shuffled down the hall and Juicebox remained slumped at the edge of the old brass bed. He sighed and stared blankly at the wall in front of him, silently vowing never to move his body again.

# Chapter 5

*"Stars, hide your fires, Let not light see my black and deep desires."*
-William Shakespeare

Time and the world froze, at least for Juicebox. He continued to just sit on the edge of his bed, unaware of anything around him. Occasionally, he could hear his grandmother talking on the phone in the hall. She tried to help him; she brought him junk food and encouraged him to go out. All the usual, surface level things that didn't even begin to soothe the wounds inside his soul. He denied any help offered and moved like a slow, haunted zombie when he did move at all.

"I don't know, Delilah, that's just how it works... I don't know what the hell you want me to do about it?" Grandma half-yelled to the phone in her hand. Juicebox knew she was talking about him. There wasn't anything he wanted anyone to do about him. He wanted to die; that was all—nothing anyone could do.

He heard her aged pink slippers dusting the floor as she moved down the hall toward his room. She cracked open his door and peeked in. He saw her old, wrinkled face caked with a creamy mask and he swallowed down a shriek at the unexpected sight. Her nightgown always hung a little too low on her shoulders and her hair seemed to be eternally wrapped in curlers with a cigarette forever dangling between her lips. Juicebox was used to Grandma's get up by now, but the face mask was new. He silently added it to the list of possible sights he might run into when he got up to grab a drink of water in the middle of the night.

Grandma carried the handpiece of her phone with a cord that stretched from the kitchen all the way down the hall. She pressed the phone to her shoulder and looked in at him sitting on the edge of the bed.

"You know, kid, you're going to leave a dent in that mattress that will sink to the floor if you don't get up some time," she said. "You need to get outside. Go out to the yard and start fixing up that old piece of junk car rusting out back or tear it apart for all I care. I don't know, go be a kid and do something!"

There was a pause, and she pressed the phone more firmly to her ear.

"No, not you, Delilah. Yes, you are looking a little run down you old bat, but I was talking to my grandson." She started to shuffle down the hall but stopped and poked her head into the room. "I'm ordering Chinese food. What do you want?"

Juicebox didn't look up. "I'm fine."

"Okay, triple orange chicken it is." The sound of slippers and Grandma cursing retreated down the hall. "Alright, Delilah, don't get your panties in a wad." Her voice trailed off the further she went.

Juicebox curled up on his bed with the room's silence pressing down on him. He didn't want to feel anything. He tried not to think, but memories always haunted his mind. A ray of late afternoon sun angled through the bedroom window and hit the bed just in front of Juicebox's face. Logic said the light was warm and cheerful. He knew he should feel something good. He just didn't believe that he deserved anything in his life that was close to good. He remembered how Stacy looked when the sun hit her hair. A tinge of hope started to tingle in his chest. Maybe...just maybe. He shut his eyes against the sun and his thoughts. He shouldn't feel good. His parents just died, after all.

The whispers started again. He wasn't sure if he invited them into his thoughts or if they took him down the path of sadness as a captive. Either way, he hated the thoughts. The hope in his chest was gone, replaced with the all too familiar sense of worthless foreboding. He wanted the voice to go away. He just didn't know how to make that happen.

Jefferson and Stacy came to visit when they could. They tried to pull him out of his gloom. But what good was it anyway? He was trash. He didn't deserve them as friends. Their visits went from happening every day to maybe once a week. His skateboard sat against the wall gathering dust.

Curled up on the bed, he felt ready to give in to the evil voice in his mind.

*"THIS IS ALL YOUR FAULT. YOU DID THIS. YOU SHOULD HAVE JUST APOLOGIZED TO YOUR MOM. YOU ARE WORTHLESS. YOU ARE NOTHING,"* the voice hissed. The words were always the same.

*"IT'S ALL YOUR FAULT. IT'S ALL YOUR FAULT. IT'S ALL YOUR FAULT!"*

The words in his mind began to throb and hurt. They trailed through the rest of his body and ached as they repeated themselves over and over, the pain seeming to grow in intensity as time marched forward. It began to settle deep in his gut, churning and gurgling. He was used to the constant, muted throbbing of this pain, but suddenly the torment was intensified and Juicebox doubled over in agony.

"AAHHH," he cried out as the pain pulsed through him like fire in his veins and brought him tumbling off his bed and onto his knees. *The bathroom. I need to get to the bathroom,* he thought frantically. *Maybe there's some medicine in the cabinet. Something, anything to help this excruciating pain.* He slid off the bed and made his way down the hall. Grandma was still talking on the phone, unaware of her grandson stumbling toward the door, clenching his stomach in agony.

Juicebox swung the bathroom door open, fumbling his way to the sink. He grasped one shaking hand to each side of it as he began to sweat and shake.

"What is this?" Juicebox felt terrified. The pain, guilt, and sadness were more than he could hold in any longer. Juicebox slowly lifted his head and stared at himself in the mirror. He challenged his own sad eyes with mental questions of why. The sharp pain in his abdomen doubled him over the sink until he caught his breath again. "Aaahh!" He yelled out, growing more frantic. He looked back up at himself in the mirror and noticed that one of his eyes was now glowing pink, and a thick purple liquid had begun to run from his nose. "What is happening to me?" Juicebox croaked, barely able to speak through the pain. Violent coughing racked him, bending him over the sink again.

"What… is… happening!" Juicebox stumbled over to the toilet.

*"Just breathe, man. Hold it together. You're just sick. You probably just need to throw up or*

*something..."* The pain grabbed hold of him again. Juicebox screamed, "AAHHH!!"

His body started to convulse out of control. The pain was like a raging wildfire that consumed his body both inside and out. Somehow he managed to stay standing. His back arched so far he thought his bones would break, and his eyes fixed on the dim ceiling light. A rotten stench seeped into the bathroom. He tried to cry out, but no sound would come. Purple slime began to flow from some unknown source on his body, oozing and dripping down his face. He gagged and tried to breathe while fighting to stay conscious as the pain brought silent, violet tears to his eyes.

With a bone-crunching snap something tore itself away from his body and the pain subsided. He looked up to find that he was not alone. He didn't know if it was a monster, a demon, or the devil himself—but towering above Juicebox was a massive figure made of darkness. A scream broke free from

Juicebox's previously stunted vocal chords and beat against the walls of the bathroom.

The monster spoke with a familiar deep voice, a cocktail of sweet, menacing chaos. The sound of the whisper that once lived only inside his mind being brought to life sent an immediate icy chill up his spine.

*"WELL, HELLO,"* it said to Juicebox. It leaned in toward his face with an enormous toothy grin that almost stretched from wall to wall. Juicebox reached and grabbed the toilet brush, the only thing he could find to arm himself, and swung at the monster.

"Get away from me!" Juicebox shouted, shaking and dripping with sweat. He held up his weapon in front of himself.

The monster's smile grew mockingly wider as he let out a chuckle at the boy's defense.

*"THAT'S A FITTING WEAPON FOR SOMEONE LIKE YOU."* The purple monster slowly leaned in, its pink glowing eyes now just inches from Juicebox's face. *"YOU'RE AFRAID, AREN'T YOU?"* Its words dripped with taunting chuckles.

The demon leaned in, close enough to tear Juicebox apart within a millisecond, giving Juicebox the perfect view of his grin, which exhibited rows of sharp jagged teeth. Dark purple sludge dripped from the sides of its mouth, from between its teeth, and pooled onto the floor below. The mouth opened impossibly wide as the monster lurched for Juicebox.

The only chance for escape was the door. Juicebox gripped the toilet brush sword and swung in all directions, while yelling with all his might, "AAHHHHH!!" The monster, surprised and curious at the boy's efforts, held off for a moment as if to see where this game might go.

Juicebox dove for the door, slipping on the hall runner, and sprinted off to his room.

*"YOU CAN'T RUN FROM ME. THERE IS NOWHERE YOU CAN HIDE THAT I CAN'T FIND YOU."*

The monster exploded through the door frame causing broken wood and pieces of wall to fly through the air. With lightning speed, it followed Juicebox into his room, leaving its disgusting mucus on everything it touched. Its slimy hand casually closed the door as its evil chuckles echoed in Juicebox's ears.

*"YOU DIDN'T LISTEN TO ME, YOU FOOL. I SAID YOU CAN'T ESCAPE ME."* Long slimy fingers grabbed at Juicebox's throat and thrust him against the wall. Juicebox snapped his eyes shut against the piercing

pink stare of the monster and tried not to breathe in the hot stink that blew across his face with every word that came from its mouth. He wriggled and twisted around, struggling to free himself, but the grasp around his neck just tightened.

*"WORTHLESS LITTLE WORM,"* it said. *"LET ME EXPLAIN WHAT'S GOING TO HAPPEN NEXT..."*

Just at that moment the bedroom door swung open and Stacy's familiar voice filled the room.

"Hey, Juicebox, hope you don't mind, but your grandma let us in. She said we could come in and surprise you."

"What the…..!?" Jefferson interrupted as he scampered backward, tripping on a box that lay strewn on the floor. Stacy looked up and screamed when she saw Juicebox kicking his feet, nearly suffocating under the firm grip of the monster. Jefferson moved into action and swung his skateboard at the beast aiming for the back of its head.

"Get out!" He screamed, as his skateboard slammed into the monster.

"Juicebox!" Stacy yelled.

In one fluid motion, the giant monster swung its massive hand, sending Jefferson violently to the ground. He landed hard against the bookcase causing piles of books to fall from its shelves and onto his head.

Stacy rushed to him. "Jefferson, are you okay?"

"I'm okay," Jefferson responded dazed, "Go help Juicebox." Stacy quickly looked around the room for the best available weapon. She saw a

flashlight poking out from under the bed. She lunged for it but missed and nudged it into a tailspin. Desperately she grabbed at it again successfully, accidentally turning the light on at the same time. The beam of light glared directly at the beast.

The monster immediately dropped Juicebox in a panic and let out a blood curdling scream. Stacy and Jefferson covered their ears from the piercing noise as the monster curved its fluid body to avoid the beam of light. It scraped and climbed up and across the ceiling like a dump truck sized spider, then angled itself back around to attack Stacy from behind.

It took her only a millisecond to understand that this monster of darkness hated the light. She stood her ground and held the flashlight steady as she moved the light to every dark corner the monster tried to hide in. It jumped across the room shrieking and squealing as it went. Then launched itself under the bed, lifting it almost to the ceiling.

Stacy blasted the beam under the bed, sending the monster into a frantic escape across the ceiling and out the window into the evening air. Purple goop trailed behind its path and pooled at the window as it slurped its way out. Juicebox laid still on the floor, stealing quick puffs of air and holding his neck as he tried to catch his breath. He forced himself to his feet and took a weak step toward the window motioning for Stacy to bring the flashlight.

"Did you see where it went? Swing the light around. The yard is a mess and has way too many places it could use for a hiding spot," he said.

"What was that thing?" Jefferson came up and joined his friends, looking out at the shadowy yard. "It had to be some kind of demon."

"I don't know," replied Juicebox.

"I have never felt so scared," added Stacy. "I was so worried about you! I can't believe we came in just when we did…or you would be dead right now." She was rambling and attempting to wipe away the tears that had pooled in her eyes before they were noticed, shaking as the adrenaline of the fight wore off. "Whatever it was, it wanted you, Juicebox."

Jefferson checked the hall. He saw Grandma's slippers resting on a footstool in the living room. He could hear her laughing at a television show.

"Your grandma didn't seem to hear anything. She's down there watching tv as if nothing just happened. The end of the world as we know it could have just been here, and she would have been oblivious to the entire thing," Jefferson breathed out, completely shocked.

"Follow me!" Juicebox exclaimed and rushed down the hall and out the backdoor. The back porch light was dim, and there was a thin layer of fog that made it almost impossible to see anything in the shadows.

Juicebox took the flashlight from Stacy and kept searching for the monster. His face was pinched with pain and panic.

"I don't know what it was," he said. His breathing was rapid and labored. "But, I have a horrible feeling it's still out there watching us."

# Chapter 6

*"Deep into that darkness peering,*
*Long I stood there*
*Wondering,*
*Fearing,*
*Doubting, dreaming dreams no mortal ever dared to dream before."*
-Edgar Allen Poe

Sleep came hard to the three friends that night, especially to Juicebox. But the sunshine peering through his window let him know that a new day had arrived and demanded to be faced.

He knew he couldn't hide away in his grandma's house forever. Even his room felt unsafe now; with a monster lurking just outside the window, and he missed too much school to stay home again anyway. Besides, he wanted to be where Jefferson and Stacy were. Last night's adventure spooked something deep inside of him and he had the faintest inkling that maybe it was better that he wasn't always alone anymore.

Juicebox dusted off his backpack and headed to school. The morning air was heavy. He couldn't shake the thought of that horribly disgusting thing out there, wandering around the town, ready to attack him or worse, someone else, at any time. He kept a furtive lookout as he walked.

Students poured into the front doors of the school, looking clean and pressed in the clothes their parents had prepped for the day. Even if that wasn't true, that's what Juicebox saw, the evidence of mothers and fathers that he no longer had. These kids chatted and smiled with each other oblivious to the gray appearance of Juicebox and the monster that he battled.

He felt an itch to find his friends as soon as possible and made his way to his locker, finally catching a glimpse of Stacy and Jefferson between the flow of kids in the packed hall. Stacy waved at him and brushed a strand of hair behind her ear. Her glowing face shone like a lighthouse for Juicebox as he swam upstream toward the safety of his friends against the current of students.

Jefferson and Stacy made their way to him at his locker as if today were any normal Monday morning at a normal school in a normal town. In that split second, Juicebox wondered if his life could or would ever be normal again. He looked around at the other students and knew the chances were slim to none.

"Can we talk about what happened last night? I can't stop thinking, and my thoughts are scaring the crap out of me." Jefferson's voice was intense even though he was trying to whisper. Juicebox grabbed a book out of his locker and slammed the door shut.

"You think too much sometimes," Juicebox tried to lighten the mood. But he couldn't stop thinking either. Juicebox looked at Jefferson, his tone serious. "I know. We need to figure this out. I don't have a good feeling." The school bell interrupted the moment. Time for class. The hallway filled with a buzzing chatter, as students shuffled to their classes. "After class, we'll figure this out." School wasn't a safe place for Juicebox anymore. He never liked school, but at least before he felt like whatever trouble happened in the halls, he was the one causing it. Now he kept looking over his shoulder, half expecting to see a huge shadow demon sneaking up behind him.

There were no seating assignments in Mrs. Gill's class. The three friends sat at desks in the back corner of the room, and Juicebox pulled the hood of his jacket over his head and hoped that the extra layer of fabric would make him invisible. It was hard for Juicebox to remember diving for frogs and stuffing the desk in front of the class with the little green "presents" for Mrs. Gill. The thoughts of that afternoon caused enough pain that Juicebox could almost forget about the monster hunting him. Jefferson could not hold onto his growing panic and quickly reminded Juicebox of the current dangers of the day.

"What are we going to do? That thing is out there right now. Right now! I can't stop thinking that it will rush up any minute and rip my face off. It feels like a horror movie!" Jefferson's voice was intense and despite his attempts at whispering, the other students began looking back at him with concern.

Juicebox intentionally leaned in closer to Jefferson. "Keep your voice down, man. It won't help anything if people hear you talking about monsters. They'll think we're crazy."

"Shouldn't we call the police or something?" Jefferson tried to whisper but still spoke way too loudly.

"The police aren't going to believe anything we say," Stacy said rolling her eyes.

"That thing was after me last night," Juicebox responded. "The attack was personal. I think I need to go find it and kill it before anyone gets hurt."

Mrs. Gill exploded into the classroom, demanding everyone's attention. She didn't look at the students or even acknowledge there were students in the room. She squawked out commands as she stomped toward her desk at the front of the class.

"Quiet, everyone," she barked. She hated the chattering noise of the classroom just before the bell rang. "Open your textbooks to where we left off last class," she continued. "Becky, you can start the reading first."

Becky looked up uncomfortably. She had been in other classes with most of the students since elementary school. Everyone knew that Becky hated to read out loud.

"Can someone else start the reading today?" Becky asked with a timid voice.

For the first time since she walked into the classroom, Mrs. Gill looked up at the students. She scanned the room with a sour expression before latching her narrowed gaze onto the trembling girl.

"You will start out the reading like you were told and I will tell you when your reading time is up. Now everyone, open your books."

The sound of pages turning rustled across the classroom. Mrs. Gill weaved slowly through the aisles between desks on the hunt for any possible misbehavior from the students who liked to cause her so much trouble. She used to love teaching, but years of battling rude and careless teenagers had worn her previous enthusiasm for her vocation down to the nub. She still loved learning about the mysteries of science, but lately, her love of science just wasn't enough to put any sort of pep into her step. Not when she was constantly surrounded by students who reminded her of the nasty, mean children she remembered from her own days at school as a young girl.

She wanted the students to like her. She wished that just once, a student would linger in the room after the bell for help with a difficult chapter. She yearned for a bright young pupil to have any semblance of desire to understand the scientific mysteries of the universe. But whenever she thought about her classes this year, all that came to mind were the smart-mouthed kids who didn't care about science or study.

Her thoughts started to linger on the mortifying pranks that were constantly pulled on her, the most recent being the frogs in her desk. Anger and humiliation surged within her, painting an ugly, bitter scowl upon her mouth.

This year that anger pointed toward an all-too-confident Stacy Johnson and her cohort Juicebox. What kind of a name was Juicebox anyway? The little brat was finally back in class again after the death of his parents earlier that month. The slightest feeling of pity rushed over her as she thought of his tragedy but was quickly snuffed out by the remembrance of the toad that jumped directly into her face the morning she had discovered the news.

She stalked past his desk, watching and listening intently for any excuse to scold him or his friends as she walked by. Juicebox, Stacy, and Jefferson hated their science class, but they were smart enough to look interested in their textbooks as Mrs. Gill passed them.

When Mrs. Gill was three desks down the aisle, Stacy leaned to whisper to Juicebox. "Juicebox, look!"

He glanced at Stacy from under his jacket hood. She motioned upward with her eyes.

"Look at the ceiling!" Jefferson and Juicebox followed the direction of Stacy's gaze and stared in horror at the ceiling just above Mrs. Gill's desk. Purple ooze pooled from above the ceiling tiles and seeped through its small cracks. A large drip formed, ready to fall onto the floor in front of the desk. The interruption was just what Mrs. Gill was waiting for. She spun around to challenge her three least favorite students.

With red hot anger burning through her eyes, she fired out, "Ms. Johnson, I have told you a thousand times. Do not interrupt my class." At this point, Becky had stopped reading. Several students tried to look back at the scene beginning to form in the room without calling any attention to themselves. Watching Stacy and Juicebox get in trouble again was better than reading any day.

Mrs. Gill walked to the front of the class, ready to spew a lecture at the students. She stood directly under the swelling, purple drip that hung from the ceiling. As she turned to face the students, she slapped her palm with the ruler she picked up off the desk, her glare directed entirely toward Stacy. Stacy jumped from her chair. She didn't like her teacher any more than Mrs. Gill liked her, but the ooze posed a threat too great, even for Mrs. Gill. Stacy had to do something before the potentially poisonous drip fell onto the teacher's head.

"Mrs. Gill! Look!" Stacy tried to get the teacher to listen.

"Not another word! I am in no mood for any more of your pranks." Mrs. Gill put her hands on her hips to emphasize her meaning. The kids watched and held their breath as the pooling drip stretched downward on the verge of breaking loose.

"Please, Mrs. Gill! Watch out!" Stacy started to rush to the front of the room.

"I have had just about enough of you, Ms. Johnson!" The teacher looked as if she would explode with anger as she slapped the ruler on her hand again. With a pop, the drip burst free from the ceiling as if in slow motion, then splashed on her head and slowly poured down the side of her ears. Her pinched eyes widened with confusion then morphed back to their usual anger-filled position in a split second when she reached up to feel the warm, sticky slime on her head.

She raised a shaking finger toward Stacy. "You! No more! I am done with you!" She barked.

Stacy shook her head in desperation. "Mrs. Gill, this isn't a prank. We didn't do this."

Mrs. Gill scrubbed her face with her cardigan in an attempt to wipe away the goo. "I've heard enough! You are going to detention for the rest of the school year. I want you out of my class!" Angry spit flew from her mouth, and the warts on her chin bobbed as she yelled.

With a huff, she shakily slammed herself down at her desk to write a blistering note to the principal condemning the three students she felt were responsible for everything wrong in her world.

"Everyone, start working on the discussion questions for this chapter. I need to get the janitor to clean up this mess before the ceiling falls in." Mrs. Gill looked up at the ceiling for the first time to see the swelling spot where the ooze was coming from. "Who knows what toxic waste this mess is? When I get back, you three are coming with me to the office."

She walked out of the class attempting to hold her head high, not wanting to show those terrible brats the humiliation she felt inside. She breached the doorway and felt her feet falter a bit beneath her. *"Head high, Gill."* She chided herself. But her shoulders started to slump despite her efforts toward good posture as she walked down the hall. She was tired of the students, and she was tired of her job.

*"YOU'VE WASTED YOUR LIFE. NOBODY APPRECIATES YOU,"* a voice whispered in her ear. The

hallway was empty ahead of Mrs. Gill. She spun around and tried to catch the person who was talking to her.

"Who's there?" She asked. An uneasy dread coursed through her body. Feeling spooked, she walked faster to the janitor's office, occasionally looking over her shoulder to calm the uneasiness that was very quickly beginning to brew inside her.

¤¤¤

"That weird purple stuff is following us now! What does this mean? Do you think Mrs. Gill is going to be okay?" Stacy bit her nails nervously. She sat at her desk while Juicebox paced in the aisle in front of her. Jefferson sat too but couldn't keep his legs from bouncing beneath his desk like a nervous rabbit jumping in a cage.

"Does this mean the monster is here at school now?" Jefferson asked. He grew more fidgety and frantic with every passing second. His friends remained silent as they pondered his question.

Jefferson threw his hands up in surrender. "And now Mrs. Gill is infected. We don't even know what that means." The volume of his voice rose with the increase of his panic.

"Hey! Calm down," Juicebox patted his back encouragingly, ignoring the staring faces of the students surrounding them. "I have a plan. This is what we're going to do. We'll go out tonight and find this thing. I think we can lure it out to us. We'll torch it or something. Remember how it hated the light? I bet it would hate fire even more. We just have to stick together."

"The three of us," Stacy agreed.

"Okay," said Jefferson. His legs stopped bouncing. "You're right. We can do this as long as we stick together."

The door of the classroom opened as Mrs. Gill returned, with the school's Janitor, Toby, following closely behind her. Mrs. Gill stumbled in through the door, catching herself on the doorknob. She was hunched over, obviously in pain. She straightened up and looked to the back corner of the classroom where

Stacy, Jefferson, and Juicebox were watching her intently. Stacy gasped.

"Do you see her eyes?" Juicebox whispered to his friends.

"Yes," Stacy replied before Jefferson could find his voice. "The same pink glow as the monster's."

Mrs. Gill showed Toby where the ooze dripped from the ceiling.

"Hmmm. I see," he said, stroking his bushy mustache. "I'll need some plastic and a few nails to cover up that leak. Then I'll need to figure out where it's coming from." He stood there for a few moments, silently staring at the strange substance leaking from the ceiling, then set down a rusty bucket underneath the leak.

"That bucket should hold whatever drips may fall until I get back. I'll leave my mop set up in the corner for the time being." He gave one more confused glance toward the ceiling and mumbled as he headed out of the classroom to gather the supplies he needed.

Mrs. Gill tried to get back to school business and acted like nothing had happened. She walked back to her desk to open her textbook.

"I think we have had enough interruptions for the day. The three of you will follow me to the office when the bell rings. Now everyone, open up your books to where we left off before your classmates so rudely interrupted the lesson." A wave of piercing pain throbbed within her abdomen, and she smacked one hand down on the desk for support while her other hand grabbed at her stomach. This was a pain unlike anything she had felt before. Her insides felt like they were boiling — churning and gurgling deep inside of her.

"AHHH!" she yelled out. The students watched as she looked up and saw that her face was bubbling in unearthly shades of red and purple. The classroom gave a gasp of fear in unison.

"Mrs. Gill," Stacy moved to approach her. She wanted to help, but after experiencing the strength of the monster, hesitated to rush to the teacher, "Are you okay?"

"I'm... I'm... fine," the teacher mumbled. "Those boiled eggs I ate for breakfast must not have been as fresh as I thought they were." She sat down at her desk and shakily popped off the cap of her red pen as if she were about to start grading papers, then howled in pain as she hugged her stomach.

"I need my pills." Mrs. Gill's voice sounded distant and weak. She reached for the drawer on the side of the desk, but her shaking hand missed its mark. She yelled again in pain, slumping lethargically into her chair.

"It's the monster!" Juicebox stood up and clenched the sides of his desk with both hands. "It's infected Mrs. Gill." He felt frozen in place with fear.

"AHHHH!" She yelled again and clenched her stomach tighter.

"I need my medicine," Mrs. Gill said. This time, she glared at Stacy, Juicebox, and Jefferson. She managed to point a shaking finger toward the trio. "This is all your fault!" She spat with disgust.

The class was visibly scared. Everyone knew Mrs. Gill had a revenge wish on Juicebox and his friends. They just didn't think Juicebox would take his pranks to the level of hurting someone. *"Maybe his parent's accident made him a little cuckoo,"* Jamie Dawson whispered to her friend Sophia. Stacy heard the gossip and snapped at the girls. "This wasn't Juicebox. It wasn't any of us." The girls looked away embarrassed as Stacy glared at them.

    Mrs. Gill looked up from her desk. Her eyes were glowing pink, and her neck rapidly bent unnaturally to the side with a bone-snapping crunch. The class erupted into screams as they watched Mrs. Gill's body contort. This couldn't be just a prank by Juicebox. Something was terribly wrong. Students were screaming as they jumped out of their seats. People in the front of the classroom stumbled over desks to get away.

    Mrs. Gill's face began to bubble and pop as her skin turned a pasty green, covered in warts and bumps. Her entire body swelled as her clothes ripped apart, buttons popping off and shooting across the room. Large razor-sharp teeth protruded from thin frog-like lips. Students began to shove and push their way out of the classroom in a panic. Mrs. Gill's clothes hung in shreds on her grotesque body.

Now looking more like a mutant frog than a human, She opened her mouth. Huge rows of teeth slowly pushed out toward the kids. An eerily long tongue flopped free from her lips. Black sludgy tar spewed across the classroom, speckling everyone like a Jackson Pollock painting. Screams echoed through the class as students ran in every direction, but despite the chaos, Mrs. Gill, the Frog Monster stared through it all with laser focus and locked eyes on Stacy.

# CHAPTER 7

*"I was angry with my friend;*
*I told my wrath, my wrath did end.*
*I was angry with my foe:*
*I told it not, my wrath did grow.*
*And I watered it in fears,*
*Night & morning with my tears:*
*And I sunned it with smiles,*
*And with soft deceitful wiles.*
*And it grew both day and night.*
*Till it bore an apple bright.*
*And my foe beheld it shine,*
*And he knew that it was mine."*
  -William Blake

"Mrs. Gill?" Stacy breathed almost inaudibly.

The frog monster who used to be the school biology teacher growled and gurgled. Her wet green skin glistened in the cheap fluorescent lighting of the classroom. Students screamed as they ran in all directions through the maze of desks between the front of the room and the back, where Stacy stood ready for battle, eyes locked on the monster who was hunting her.

Sinewy frog legs crouched, ready for an attack. Mrs. Gill rocked back and forth, waiting for her moment. Then, without warning, the monstrous teacher leapt in the air crossing the room over the top of students and desks in one powerful jump.

Stacy intentionally watched the monster coming towards her. She waited just a split second longer before she dove to the ground with perfect timing. The monster slammed into the back wall knocking down the bulletin board covered in biology posters. She bounced off the wall like an enormous water balloon that miraculously did not pop on contact. The monster paused to shake off the blow to her head just as Juicebox, Stacy, and Jefferson ran for the classroom door. The giant frog didn't need a doorway to get to the hall, but instead made her own, as she crashed through the wall, hungry for another try at attacking Stacy.

The three friends darted down the hallway, with Jefferson nearly tripping several times as he kept looking back to see where the frog demon was.

"She's getting closer!" He yelled. He looked back again, eyes widening in terror as he saw the monster run up the wall and race toward them on the ceiling. She seemed to be moving even faster now with fewer obstacles in her way. Jefferson whipped his head back around and tried to run faster.

"We have to hurry! She's on the ceiling and catching up fast!" Stacy and Juicebox took a quick look over their shoulders, terrified as they confirmed Jefferson's assessment of the situation.

Mrs. Gill scampered in a zigzag pattern between the ceiling lights. The hallway erupted into riotous chaos. Students screamed as they ran up and down the hall, frantically pushing and shoving each other to get out of the path of the monster. Teachers peered out from their classrooms to see if the noise was some kind of emergency drill they didn't know about, then quickly slammed their doors closed after witnessing the disturbing sight. The growls of the monster running along the ceiling sent a sure message that this was not a drill. Door after door was slammed shut and locked down as the three friends ran past, with Mrs. Gill right on their heels.

Juicebox knew no one was going to swoop in and save them from this slimy, green beast. As twisted as it was, running for their lives from a monster that shouldn't exist was their reality, and he needed to find a way to save himself and his friends,

maybe even the entire town. He saw they were running to where the hallway split like a fork in the road. It gave him an idea.

"I need to find something to fight off Mrs. Gill. See that hall up ahead? You head to the main office. I'll catch up with you!"

"Juicebox, we need to stick together!" Stacy insisted.

"I'll meet you at the office. I promise!"

"Hurry!" cried Jefferson. Juicebox peeled off from the group and ran down the side hall while Stacy and Jefferson went in the opposite direction toward the main office. The monster watched her prey divide and go in different directions and for a moment wasn't sure which student she should follow. A beam of fluorescent light caught a wisp of Stacy's hair and Mrs. Gill bounded in her direction, instantly reminded of her dislike for the snarky teenage girl.

*"SHE MAKES YOU FEEL WORTHLESS! SHE THINKS YOU'RE A JOKE!"* said a voice in her ear. Mrs. Gill pounced her froggy legs toward Stacy and Jefferson with renewed intensity.

¤¤¤

In the front office of the school, was a large section of the building enclosed by a glass wall. It wasn't really a room but rather a chunk taken out of the main entrance. Inside the front office were desks and a waiting room. There were two private offices in the corner of the large glassed-in area, one for the principal and the other for the vice principal. Several secretaries worked in the office and ensured the school operations ran smoothly and on schedule, the oldest one being Ms. Gigi who had been at the school for decades. She was walking to the door of the office carrying a stack of papers so large she couldn't see over the top of it. Stacy screamed out a warning to the elderly secretary.

"Ms. Gigi! Look out!"

Ms. Gigi looked around the side of the papers and beheld the monstrous horror running down the ceiling directly toward her.

"Oh, my!" The towering stack of documents launched from her grasp as she ran into the front office area. Papers flew through the air and settled on the ground as if a blizzard had blown through the school. Jefferson and Stacy darted through the paper storm trying to make it to the office. Jefferson managed to squeeze quickly through the door, but Stacy slipped on the fallen papers and landed on her back. Ms. Gigi slammed the door behind Jefferson. He pounded on the glass and yelled for Stacy to get up, but she was completely dazed by the fall.

Mr. Gary, the vice principal, was at the window where he made his morning announcements when the frog monster caught up to where Stacy was on the ground. Drool dripped to the floor as Mrs. Gill flashed a menacing grin. Before Stacy could move, Mrs. Gill fell from the ceiling and towered over the girl. Mr. Gary almost dropped the announcement microphone when he saw those horrible teeth. As scared as he was, he noticed something familiar about the monster. He thought he recognized the shredded dress hanging off her back.

"Edna? Is that you?" He asked through the intercom system. The microphone shook uncontrollably in his hand. The monster looked confused and stared up at Mr. Gary with her pink glowing eyes which blinked out of sync from each other. Jefferson screamed and pounded the glass a few panes down, trying to get the monster's attention away from Stacy.

*"IT'S THE GIRL! SHE DID THIS! SHE TURNED YOU INTO THIS THING TO MAKE A FOOL OUT OF YOU!"* The voice nagged. The monster snapped its gaze back to Stacy without distraction and slowly started to lean toward the girl, opening her mouth to show a gaping hole filled with teeth.

*"YOU! IT'S ALWAYS YOU. EVERY YEAR IT'S YOU,"* the monster hissed. *"THE NOTES YOU ALWAYS PASS BEHIND MY BACK. THE CONSTANT INTERRUPTIONS AND DISRESPECT! AND THE FROGS!!!! YOU TURNED THE ENTIRE CLASS AGAINST ME."* The monster gargled its words and inched closer to Stacy. Stacy pulled herself as close to the office wall as she could.

*"IT WAS SUPPOSED TO BE A GOOD YEAR! IT WOULD HAVE BEEN A GOOD YEAR. BUT YOUUUUUU!"* The monster was so close Stacy could smell the swampiness of her breath, rotten like sewer sludge. Mrs. Gill opened her mouth and leaned in to bite off Stacy's head. The dark drool dripped from her teeth and pooled all over the floor. Toby the Janitor hung around the corner watching, fixated on the slimy

floor and began thinking up detailed plans as to how he was going to clean up the goopy mess.

The office door flew open with a shattering bang.

"HEY! Mrs. Gill!" Jefferson yelled out trying to get the monster's attention. He was in the hall behind her wielding a fire extinguisher.

"No, wait!" Stacy jumped up and tried to stop Jefferson but was too late. Mrs. Gill suddenly turned to look at Jefferson and was met with a mouth full of fire-retardant foam.

Juicebox came up the hall at the same time. He rode the school's floor waxing machine at full speed toward the monster, but this was no typical riding waxer. This was Toby the Janitor's pride and joy. It was basically a go-cart that also could clean— <u>definitely</u> not district approved equipment.

Juicebox slammed into the monster, sending her into the wall across the hallway. She hit the wall so hard that bricks crumbled down on top of her. The monster looked stunned, then shook her head and started to get up. With pure rage, she clawed at the wall, intent to climb back to the ceiling, sending more bricks to the floor. She roared and screamed words that no one could understand. As she pulled herself up from the floor, her claw mistakenly nudged the fire alarm. Sirens sounded instantly, and sprinklers sprayed water from the ceiling. Juicebox and his friends instinctively shielded their heads with their arms and looked away from Mrs. Gill. Jefferson looked up, and the beast was gone.

"Where did she go?" he asked.

"I can't see her," replied Juicebox as he looked around. All three friends panted and tried to catch their breath as they huddled closer together. There was still the feeling that something bad lurked around the corner, waiting for them.

A screeching roar rang out, and Mrs. Gill dropped down from overhead right in front of the three students. Jefferson and Juicebox grabbed any kind of debris they could find on the floor to fight the monster off with. Stacy stepped in front of them with arms

spread wide.

"Wait!" She yelled. "We need to stop hurting her."

Juicebox was pumped with adrenaline. Stacy didn't make any sense to him. "What do you mean wait? We need to kill this monster now!"

Stacy turned to look at the frog monster who used to be her biology teacher, catching Juicebox and Jefferson completely off guard. Confused, they lowered their weapons. Stacy started to talk to the monster as if she were still Mrs. Gill, the teacher.

"This really is our fault, isn't it?" She asked. "At least partly our fault." The monster leaned in closer, her mouth still stretched wide. "I'm sorry, Mrs. Gill. I've never really cared about how any of my teachers felt. I didn't care how I was making you feel." She inhaled a shaky breath to steady herself. "It always feels like my teachers hate me. Maybe it's how I dress. Maybe it's my attitude. I don't know. But I struggle at school, and I struggle at home." Stacy looked down, embarrassed. "It's not your fault, but I take it out on you anyway."

The monster started to close her mouth and took a step back from Stacy.

"It was wrong of me to laugh at you, Mrs. Gill. And to pass notes in your class. And to pull pranks on you. Nobody deserves to be made fun of. I guess I thought nothing I did could really hurt you. But I see now that that isn't true. I made a mistake and I hope you can forgive me," She finished her speech, and the monster let out an ear-piercing screech in response. It was as if Stacy's words caused the monster real physical pain.

They both stood there for a moment as the water sprayed above, just looking at each other. All of a sudden, Mrs. Gill made a giant leap, bursting through the wall of the school and ran out of the building. The three friends stood in the wet hallway and said nothing amidst the alarms and sprinklers.

Juicebox broke the silence. "What just happened?"

"That was insane," Jefferson said.

"I think the monster feeds on emotions. We shouldn't have been so mean to her," Stacy said.

"The monster we saw at my house did this," Juicebox added. "It seems like the ooze is spreading. It could be making its way around the entire town."

"Damn." Jefferson ran a hand through his hair. "Do you think we will have a sub tomorrow in

Biology?" Stacy and Juicebox let out a small laugh. Juicebox kicked at some of the rubble on the ground and peered down the beaten path of the hallway. The school was completely destroyed.

"I don't think we'll be coming to school tomorrow."

"I just want to get out of here," Stacy said as she stared through the monster-sized hole in the wall leading to the schoolyard. Students and teachers wandered out of classrooms. Mr. Gary walked around acting like either a small-town hero or the boss of a construction site as he gave orders and directions to everyone.

"You guys can stay at my place tonight," Juicebox said. "My grandma won't mind. You can call your parents when we get there."

Juicebox, Jefferson, and Stacy stood close to each other as they emerged from the school through the gaping hole in the wall. They didn't notice the pink glowing eyes in the trees all around them as they walked down the street to Juicebox's grandmother's house.

*"There are sleeping dreams and waking dreams;
What seems is not always as it seems."*
*-Christina Rosetti*

Juicebox stared out his bedroom window while Jefferson paced back and forth in the small space in front of the bed behind him. Jefferson's adrenaline levels were over-the-top, unable to sit still for the life of him. Stacy was quiet on the floor in front of the bed. She rhythmically spun a wheel on the skateboard that was turned upside down on her lap. She closed her eyes and took a deep breath.

The attempt to block out the memory of the giant frog beast trying to bite off her head didn't work. She could still smell the stench of the swampy breath blowing in her face from the monstrous mouth of Mrs. Gill. All three of the kids felt the shock of having a school-teacher-turned-monster try to kill them at the beginning of what should have been a normal school day. The unspoken question they were all trying to grapple with was, what they were supposed to do now.

"Can you believe what just happened? That whole thing was just crazy! I mean, BEYOND CRAZY!" Jefferson's pacing increased the more he spoke. He talked without taking a breath, making frantic statements as he processed out loud, directing his comments to nobody in particular. "We almost died. Man, I almost died. This can't be real. Is this really happening?"

"Jefferson, Slow down! I can't think. I need to figure out what to do. We have to do something. I think people are going to get hurt," Juicebox said. He lowered his voice, "This is somehow all my fault."

Jefferson stopped pacing between his friends and looked up at Juicebox with pleading eyes, "Do you think you know what these monsters are?"

Juicebox felt the acidic pit inside his stomach start to churn. "I might have an idea. I'm not completely sure, but… I really do think this is all my fault." Juicebox looked at the floor. He avoided the intense eyes of his friends searching for answers. If he was to blame, Juicebox had to own the responsibility of hurting his teacher, scaring his friends, destroying the school, and putting the entire town in danger. The guilt from this responsibility made his heart beat so hard it hurt. If only he could just go to sleep and wake up in a different world.

He turned away from his friends and looked out the window again. So much had happened. Despite it only being midday, he noticed that the sky was darkening and wondered if a storm was coming. Rain wouldn't wash away the heavy feelings he carried. In just the past few weeks, his parents were gone, a monster ripped out of his body, and he was almost killed by his science teacher.

Stacy stood up and put her hand on Juicebox's shoulder. He didn't turn around but kept staring out the window.

"Just tell us what you think is going on. You know you can trust us with anything."

Juicebox turned to face his friends. "Remember last night when you found me being choked by that monster?"

"How could we forget that freak show?" Jefferson shook his head in disbelief at remembrance of the previous night. Stacy nodded in agreement. Juicebox took a deep breath and continued with his story.

"Well, before you saved me, I wasn't feeling like myself."

"Like sick? Or something else?" Jefferson interrupted.

"I'm not sure how to explain it. I haven't always told you guys when I'm feeling off, even before my parents died. I'm not even sure if "off," is even the right word. It's hard to explain sometimes," Juicebox sniffed and wiped at a tear with his sleeve. "Everything was technically okay before the accident. I shouldn't have had anything to complain about. Nothing was actually wrong — but somehow I still felt wrong inside. I never wanted to get out of bed. I was having a hard time wanting to do anything at all.

Even video games and comics didn't make me fully happy anymore."

Juicebox shook his head at himself. "I should have been happy when my life was perfectly fine. It just goes to show how messed up I am, and how ungrateful I've been. What kind of kid feels miserable when nothing is even wrong in his life?" He gritted his teeth in anger at himself. "I guess now I am getting what I deserve. I thought life sucked before. Well, now life is showing me just how terrible things can really be. It's just too much… I'm not just sad. I'm more than sad. I feel… saggy." He stared out the window again. "I don't know if that makes sense. Everything just hurts. Moving, thinking, even breathing. It all just hurts so much. I don't know how I can keep going."

Stacy snuggled up to Juicebox on the bed and leaned in, wrapping her arms around him.

"I think I know what you're feeling. I feel the same type of hurt sometimes. That same type of *sagginess*. It started for me after my dad left. It hurt so much I felt like I couldn't get out of bed in the morning. You know how I skip school a lot? I know what it feels like to just want to hide and sleep everything away," Stacy's eyes glazed over as if they were focused on something in the distance.

Jefferson quietly added his thoughts to the discussion. "I feel it sometimes too. My parents push me so hard in everything. It feels like the only thing that matters to them is grades, building a resume, and being some hot shot business guy someday. Future this! And future that! I can't make any decisions for myself or have an opinion about anything. No breaks. I can't breathe most days. My stomach is a constant churning pot of nerves. It's getting harder to keep going." Juicebox patted a reassuring hand on Jefferson's back as the three friends sat for a moment in their thoughts.

"So, what happened with this monster?" Stacy urged Juicebox to continue with his story.

"Well, like I said, I wasn't feeling myself. I was in that saggy pit of despair when this physical pain completely overtook me. The pain was so bad, it doubled me over. I couldn't breathe. I thought if I could just get to the bathroom and splash some water on my face, I could calm down. I barely made it to the bathroom, almost fell so many times, and couldn't find any pain medicine to help. Water didn't do anything. And then I heard a voice, laughing and taunting me, and all of a sudden...this Thing...that Monster ripped out of me." His friends' eyes widened with shock.

"Whoaaah..." Jefferson exclaimed. Stacy stammered unsure of what to say.

"This sounds like some next-level comic book stuff," Jefferson said.

Juicebox sat forward on the edge of the bed, elbows on his knees, his head dropped lower towards the floor. He couldn't look at his friends for fear that the unleashing of this secret had pushed them away. He knew that would be the ultimate hurt that would unravel him permanently.

"I can't think of any other good explanation as to where this monster came from but me. I'm more than sure I created that beast, and now everyone is paying for it."

The room was quiet as Stacy and Jefferson processed the new information.

"Juicebox, you might be right. Maybe the monster really did come out of you somehow. But I don't know if that means this is all really your fault. It's not like you had any control over that thing. And it definitely wasn't something that you were trying to make happen. Who knows, it could have happened to any one of us," Jefferson tried to reassure Juicebox. "Let's assume that monster really did come from your sadness or whatever. Does that mean it's part of you in some way?"

Juicebox sunk a little deeper into his guilty gloom, his shoulders dropping with the weight of the responsibility for all that was wrong in the town.

"Juicebox, this isn't your fault." Stacy reached a hand to her friend and raised his chin upward. "Look at me and hear me. This isn't your fault," she said. "Everything will be okay. You know why?" She forced him again to meet her eyes. "We're in this together. And we will fight together to make sure that everything is okay. Which means that you'll be okay, too. Are you listening to me?" She looked at Jefferson for confirmation. He nodded his head emphatically.

"She's right, Juice. We'll beat this together," Jefferson added. Juicebox nodded, trying to gather some strength from his friends' words.

A loud roar cut their conversation short as it ripped through the air from somewhere outside. The three friends jumped at the noise and looked at each other startled by the sound. The safety bubble they created with talk of togetherness was popped by the loud buzz of an emergency announcement that sounded from the television in the living room. They ran down the hall to find Juicebox's grandma snoring in her recliner. A diet cola was balanced carefully in her hand. The announcement hadn't bothered her naptime at all.

**ANCHORMAN**: *We interrupt this program with emergency information.*

The kids held their breath to hear if this announcement had anything to do with Mrs. Gill running around town, causing destruction.

**ANCHORMAN**: *Citizens are turning into mutated monsters all over town. The cause of these mutations is related to a mysterious purple liquid. It is still unclear where this substance is coming from.*

*Monsters, yes you heard that right, monsters are attacking citizens. Reports of new attacks and sightings are coming in from every section of the town. We urge all citizens to stay inside. Do not touch or get close to this unknown substance. We will keep the town informed of any new developments.*

Juicebox looked at Jefferson. Jefferson turned to Stacy.

"I need to go out there and figure this out." Juicebox sighed. "You guys don't have to come with me, in fact you should probably stay here inside where it's safe. But this has something to do with me, and I need to make it right."

Jefferson ran an anxious hand through his hair and Stacy rolled her eyes. "You're not doing this alone, Juicebox." She took a deep breath and shot her eyes toward Jefferson. "Right Jefferson?" Jefferson turned to face the tv and pinched at the bridge of his nose as he watched the disturbing images of the outside world flash across the screen.

Stacy stepped in front of him. "Right, Jefferson?!?!?" Jefferson groaned. "Of course not." He shook his head with dread and Juicebox walked toward the window to look outside.

He was determined to fix this. Juicebox clenched his fists and scrunched his face as he pushed his saggy feelings down deep into his gut. He had a job to do and he needed to focus. Stacy went to the closet and found an old baseball bat, turning it in her hands as she tested its grip. "This is perfect," she said to herself.

Juicebox rummaged through the kitchen junk drawer. He gathered duct tape and scissors and grabbed the hammer that was stuck behind decades worth of pencils, paper clips and rubber bands. Jefferson went for the hockey stick that rested in the corner behind Juicebox's bedroom door. They found cardboard from old pizza boxes in the garbage and taped it around their shins with duct tape and made sure to grab some flashlights as well.

Thoughts of battles with monsters, purple slime, and razor-sharp teeth ran rampant through their thoughts. They had no clear plan in place. No guidebook or roadmap, just a faint glow of courage and the pull within themselves to try. The friends marched down the hall together toward the front door. Jefferson grabbed the umbrellas from the stand next to the door and handed one to each person.

"What's this for?" Juicebox asked him.

"Didn't you see out your window?"

Juicebox looked at him, confused. They stepped out onto the front porch. Jefferson smiled smugly at Juicebox. "See what I mean?"

The darkened sky that brooded earlier had now turned into a full-on storm. Dark clouds swirled and expanded like a bomb had gone off in the sky. They seemed to drop lower and lower with every passing moment giving the friends a feeling of claustrophobia. Pink lightning zapped through the clouds igniting the town in a hazy glow. Purple rain began to drizzle and drop all over everyone and everything uncovered outside. The wind was blowing, making the trees dance and sway as the sound of leaves rustling filled the neighborhood.

Juicebox took a deep breath and swallowed the lump that had formed in his throat. "Let's do this."

*"In this short life that only lasts an hour
How much - how little - is within our power."*
*-Emily Dickinson*

    Juicebox looked around at the chaos that was once his quiet neighborhood. He caught a view of a woman who was walking her dog across the street. She slumped down and seemed to stumble when a pile of dark violet goo fell on her head. Her dog barked intensely as if his owner was now someone else, pulling frantically on the leash, trying to make his escape.

    A man came home from work a few houses down the street. He got out of his car and ran toward his house with a briefcase held up to protect his head from the storm. A large purple drip thwarted his sprint and landed directly on top of his hand. He stopped in his tracks and slumped over like the woman with the dog.

A handful of children rode their bikes down the sidewalk, excitedly giggling to be out in the rain. As they passed, one of the kids tipped back her head and stuck out her tongue to catch a candy-colored raindrop from the sky. Her bike swerved to a crash. The girl stood up and looked over at the three friends on the porch with glowing pink eyes.

Everyone touched by the storm drooped and sagged. Mouths hung open in distorted ways; eyes glowed like strange bugs in a midnight forest. The atmosphere had an eerie feeling as if the unnatural storm was settling in for a long, turbulent season.

"Did you see that?!" Jefferson couldn't stop pointing at the zombie-like changes the kids were witnessing. His eyes darted down the street until his gaze landed on his own house. It looked small in the distance but was surrounded by an extra menacing looking cloud which seemed to be flinging buckets of purple mud down from the sky. The ooze built up heavily on Jefferson's house. In a matter of seconds, the kids watched as half the roof collapsed over the garage.

"My house!" Jefferson screamed. "I have to go check on my parents! Dad should be home from work by now." He ran from the porch without thinking about any danger of contamination.

"Jefferson! Wait!" Juicebox shouted and followed after him. "We can't let any of this crap get on us. Be careful!"

Jefferson pulled his jacket over his head and steadied his umbrella, continuing his sprint toward his home. Stacy and Juicebox followed, dodging pink-eyed neighbors that seemed to be increasing by the second.

Jefferson's face looked tense, with lines etched deeply onto his brow. It was one thing to watch your teacher turn into a monster, but Jefferson couldn't imagine his parents attacking him... unless it was about his grades of course.

The block distance to the house felt like miles, even running on heart-pounding adrenaline. Every ticking second was like a metronome beat of worry in the kids' minds, not knowing what they would find at

Jefferson's house. The sickening stench of the slimy rain filled the air and burned their throats.

They ran up the front yard and burst through the door. Jefferson slid in on the entryway tile with Juicebox and Stacy at his heels. Jefferson could see from the doorway that his mom was standing at the kitchen counter scrubbing dishes in the sink. The peaceful normalcy of the sight brought a rush of relief to Jefferson's chest. He quickly moved to step into the kitchen and then halted in his tracks. Something was off. His mom's movements were unsettlingly mechanical. *Scrub. Scrub. Scrub, rinse, repeat.*

"Mom?" Jefferson called out to her, unsure of the woman in front of him. His mom turned quickly to put the newly cleaned dishes away. Just before her back disappeared behind the wall, Jefferson noticed a long stream of purple ooze running down her neck.

"MOM!" Jefferson screamed. Jefferson took an instinctive step back away from the kitchen. It was dead silent. The three friends began to slowly back up as well when they heard an irritated voice boom from the kitchen. "Jefferson!" his mom shouted, popping out from the connected living room. "You're late."

She said as her eyes flickered pink then faded back to normal.

"Mom?" Jefferson was in shock. How could this happen to his parents? His mom's expression turned menacing. Her usually prim and proper demeanor morphed into monstrous anger. "You're late!!" She yelled again as her jaw stretched like a broken puppet distorting her face. "Get upstairs and get your homework done!"

Jefferson's hands were trembling. "Mom? I think something is wrong with you."

"NOW!" She commanded. "Don't ever talk to me like that again! Nothing is wrong with me besides the irritation I constantly feel from being forced to tell you how to behave! You have until the count of 3 to get yourself up those stairs and into your room. One… two…." As she counted, her face continued to shift and change. Her skin melted like a hot wax candle. Jefferson turned and ran up the stairs to his room.

Juicebox and Stacy stood in the entryway, unsure of what to do. If Jefferson's mom attacked them, they would have to fight something that used to be the person who gave them homemade cookies on normal stormy days. They didn't want to think about the possibility of hurting Jefferson's mom. Her face went back to normal, and she walked off, continuing to straighten up the house while she hummed.

Juicebox and Stacy headed up the stairs slowly and silently. A noise in the living room stopped their escape. Jefferson's dad walked towards them, "No friends over right now," He began to speak. "Jefferson needs to finish his homework." His eyes glowed as he turned to walk away from them. Stacy pushed Juicebox up the stairs, and they bolted away from the obviously infected parents.

Just as they reached Jefferson's bedroom door, they heard his mom call up to him. Her sticky sweet voice caused a creepy chill to crawl up their spines. "Jefferson, honey, I'll be up in a few minutes to check on how your homework is going." Stacy closed the door to the bedroom. Jefferson rushed to his desk and opened his math book, sticking a pencil in his mouth and chewing on it nervously as he began to work on the problems scrawled across the page.

"Jefferson, we need to get out of here!" Stacy said, trying to snap him out of his homework-induced panic. Only Jefferson's rapidly bouncing leg, jerking up and down a million times a minute under his desk gave any indication that something more was happening with him. His parents had clearly begun their transition into monsters, but Jefferson was responding as if this was a regular fear and command. His attention was focused intently on his algebra book, doing his homework, just like his mom told him to do.

Juicebox patted his friend gently. "Jefferson, you can't be thinking about doing homework right now. That stuff infected your parents, and now your house is about to cave in on itself. We need to go. I'm really sorry, man. Really, I am." The acrid smell of infection was getting stronger as the ceiling and walls groaned. The house could collapse at any minute. Jefferson looked at the ceiling and thought about how much time they had to get out.

"Monsters or not, I need to do what my parents say. If I don't, who knows what they'll do to me. I've never been in trouble with monster dad before but if he's anything like my real dad, I sure don't want to find out. If you haven't noticed, my grades and school are the most important things to my parents. Maybe even more important than… me." Jefferson kept his eyes on the book and frantically tried to solve each problem.

It was strange but with each problem he solved he felt a small amount of relief. Not because he was getting closer to finishing the work and ensuring he'd please his parents, but because he felt like he was solving pieces of his life. Pretending his life was one big math problem was one of Jefferson's favorite things to do. Because if it were, he knew he could solve it.

"We know," said Stacy. "You're a hard worker, Jefferson. But we need to go now. Bring the book with you if it helps you feel better."

"I gotta do this now. I'll pay for it later if I don't get this homework done," Jefferson pointed and tapped his finger at the opened page of the algebra book for emphasis. "How's the homework coming, Jefferson?" a demonic voice boomed from downstairs. "Think, think, think…" Jefferson began to chant and shake as he tried to force himself to be quick. The stress and intensity spun Jefferson into some sort of panic attack. His heart pounded, and a painful lump formed in the back of his throat. As his jaw clenched tighter and tighter, his nose began to bleed. But not with red blood. A thick purple sludge dripped from Jefferson's nose and fell onto the math book pages below. The book began to shake with a gentle tremor.

"I didn't do that," Jefferson said as he leaned back a little from the book with his hands raised as if he was facing the barrel of a gun. Stacy and Juicebox stepped backward as the book started to shake again, rattling with increasing violence. It spun around and snapped open and closed, like the hungry jaws of a vicious piranha. The friends all flinched with each chomp of the book until it forced itself closed in an eerie and sudden silence.

"What....!?" Jefferson leaned in toward the book to examine it more closely. The book suddenly tore itself open with a screech and Jefferson flung himself back from his desk chair. Out of the pages flew an endless swarm of blue monsters the shape and size of squishy beach balls. They poured from the pages like water from a hose, flying out by the hundreds with such force that many of them splattered on the bedroom ceiling.

The bodies of the bulbous monsters wriggled and bounced, while their vicious mouths flapped and snarled, making a clear show of their jagged and grotesque teeth which chomped and tore into everything they could snatch. Their long, floppy, noodle-like arms swung and swayed like dangling branches from weeping willow trees as they flew hectically around the room. Their constant clacking of gnashing teeth added to the noise of the room as they ripped pillows, window blinds, and furniture. Feathers and sawdust fell around the three friends as they stood in shock, taking in the wreckage of the moment.

"We have to do something!" Stacy screamed.

Jefferson stood in shock, seemingly forgetful that his friends were standing behind him as his private space and home imploded. Monsters were pouring out of the book so fast that the room was losing capacity to hold them all, and a few of the bulbous beasts were now flying quickly toward the friends with mouths opened wider than their size should allow.

"Look out!" Stacy yelled as she wound up her bat. Right as a monster flew within range, she released her swing and SPLAT! Her bat sent the blue thing soaring across the room, where it exploded against the bedroom wall.

Juicebox dove into the fight with fury. He kicked, punched, and battled monsters on all sides, bashing the teeth out from some of the demons with his hammer as he spun around in a frenzy.

"We have to get out of here!" Jefferson announced.

"No kidding!" Stacy yelled back sarcastically as she swung at another monster, pushing forward toward Jefferson. "It's time to go." She grabbed Jefferson's arm and jerked him towards the door. The three kids fell out of the room, and Jefferson kicked the door shut. It shook violently with the swarm of monsters behind it.

"I…I…." Jefferson couldn't get any words out.

"I know," said Juicebox. "Losing your life as you know it hurts more than anything. Come on. We have to leave now before the house collapses. I'm sorry, man. We can cry together later. Right now, we've gotta run."

A demonic voice trailed up the stairs from the kitchen. "Jefferson? Is your homework finished? YOU NEED TO DO YOUR ALGEBRA!"

When the kids didn't reply, her voice changed to a deep guttural growl.

"Jefferson! College applications are due in three years! AAAGGHHHHH! But I don't think you will make the DEADLINE!" She growled and stumbled out of the kitchen. Her face bubbled and sagged as her eyes grew large and glowed with that familiar sickly pink. The three kids ran swiftly past her and out the front door, followed by a wave of blue monsters. The friends jumped onto their skateboards as the demons filled the neighborhood, most of the swarm flying toward their escaping prey.

In the short time the three of them had been inside the house, the purple rainstorm had ceased, but chaos had continued to take over the outside world. Men and women who should have been returning to their homes from work for the day, were clambering out of their vehicles as newly mutated beasts, and uninfected citizens screamed as they ran down the street, trying to escape the mayhem. In the distance, police sirens and car alarms sounded loudly, adding to the noise and craze of the community.

Juicebox glanced at his friends who both had their eyes glued to Jefferson's house. Large kraken-like tentacles had burst out of the chimney and windows and the garage had finally caved in on itself completely. Jefferson had both hands to his face shaking his head in disbelief. "My parents!" He cried out. Juicebox and Stacy hugged him tightly as they took in the horrific scene.

The blue monsters were getting closer and they were going to have to start running again. "I'm so sorry Jefferson," Stacy cried into his shoulder. "Wait…" He breathed out. Juicebox and Stacy both looked up and saw Jefferson's parents walk out of the distorted front door of the home. They had definitely been fully mutated into monsters but were still alive.

Jefferson seemed content to start running again after making sure that his parents had made it out of the house okay. He glanced to his right and noticed that the swarm of enemies were now just a few yards away. The loud warning horn of a bus blared at the trio as it barreled down the middle of the street toward them.

Jefferson, Stacy, and Juicebox scrambled to push hard off on their skateboards to the other side of the street to dodge the oncoming danger. It passed them by with perfect timing to stop the swarm of monsters that were just moments away from ripping the kids to shreds. The flying beasts popped like pesky bugs exploding on a windshield against the side of the bus.

"We need to find a place to hide. Now is our only chance," Jefferson seemed to be coming out of his shock. He looked around to find any place where they could be safe from the rest of the swarming hoard. "There!" he pointed.

At the edge of the neighborhood on the corner was the Miller family's house. Mr. Miller wanted to stop people from cutting across the edge of his grass instead of walking the entire corner of the sidewalk, so he built a decorative wall around the corner of his yard. There was a place where the wall stood next to a row of overgrown bushes that made a small alley-like path by the street that led into the backyard. The three kids raced behind the wall, just in front of the bushes before the rest of the monsters could catch up to them. They flew by, not detecting their hidden victims crouching just out of view.

Once the monsters had passed, Juicebox stood up and took in the view of the neighborhood. The strange color of the sky in the distance enhanced the plumes of smoke that rose from all over town. While some of the neighbors seemed to have shifted into aggressive beasts, upon further inspection of the townspeople, he noticed that not everyone had become a raging monster when infected. Some people just looked saggy, like melting wax, with a sadness that sapped them of their energy or ability to do anything but walk forward like zombies, dragging their feet as their hands hung down low by their sides. Some of them sat slumped in their yards or in the middle of the street.

"*JUICEBOX... JUICEBOX....*" came a menacing whisper from the alley behind him. The voice had a false sweetness to it that made Juicebox's skin crawl. He whipped around to look behind him. In the shadows, he saw the familiar grin, full of teeth and two glowing pink eyes.

"*LOOK AT YOU... IT'S JUST SO CUTE WATCHING YOU TRY TO FIX THIS BIG MESS YOU'VE MADE,*" the darkness hissed at him. "*YOU DO KNOW YOUR EFFORTS ARE POINTLESS, RIGHT? TELL ME, WHAT MAKES YOU BELIEVE THAT A WORTHLESS WORM LIKE YOU COULD MAKE ANY OF THIS BETTER?*" The voice continued to grow in intensity and viciousness as it rattled on. "*YES, KEEP ON TRYING TO CLOSE THE BOX YOU'VE UNLEASHED LITTLE PANDORA...*" Juicebox put his hands to his ears and the voice halted for a moment.

"*IF ONLY YOUR PARENTS COULD SEE THE POSITIVE MARK THEIR ONLY SON WAS LEAVING ON THE WORLD.*" The darkness cruelly taunted.

A hand on his shoulder snapped him back to reality.

"Juice, are you okay?" Stacy stared at him with concern in her eyes and Juicebox turned from the darkness.

"Uhhh... Yeah, I'm good. I just thought I heard something. Thought I saw something, too." Stacy linked her arms through each of her friends' and urged them out of the alley and back to the road.

"Well," she said, "Looks like we made it through day one of the apocalypse. Do you think we could still find some pizza somewhere?"

They all watched, their feet glued to the street as a large, scaled monster in the distance flew across the sky, its loud screech echoing through the town. Plumes of smoke from smoldering fires dotting the horizon burned at their noses, and glowing eyeballs followed them down the street.

"Okay," Stacy breathed, "So maybe no pizza tonight."

# CHAPTER 10

*"For I have known them all already, known them all:*
*Have known the evenings, mornings, afternoons,*
*I have measured out my life with coffee spoons;*
*I know the voices dying with a dying fall*
*Beneath the music from a farther room.*
*So how should I presume?"*
-T.S. Elliot

Juicebox led his friends down the middle of Main Street. They flew down the road like shooting stars, swerving past abandoned vehicles and debris on their boards. There was nowhere they could turn that wasn't filled with strange and eerie sights. At one point, the three passed by a taxi whose driver had somehow melded himself into the car. He clutched permanently at the steering wheel and wailed loudly out the window with complaints of a broken engine.

The friends shuddered as they continued down the road and past the park. There was a man calling out to them from the grassy field who walked toward them slowly with his long, noodle-like arms trailing on the ground behind him. He made an effort to jump into the street as they passed, nearly causing Jefferson to stumble off his board, but the friends made a quick escape from the monster due to his snail-like speed.

As they got closer to town, their skateboard wheels seemed to stick to the pavement. Stacy was the first to jump off and inspect her board.

"Something is wrong with the road," she said.

Jefferson inspected the bottom of his shoe and shot a curious look at Juicebox. "What do you think is happening?" He asked.

"I don't know," Juicebox stared at the pavement and pondered. "The ground is changing. I'm guessing the people aren't the only ones getting infected by this stuff. I think the earth is sick, too." They all felt a low rumble coming from deep under the street. It shook the road like an earthquake. Stacy grabbed Jefferson's arm to steady herself as they wobbled like Jello in the wind.

Suddenly, the road split down the middle with an ear-piercing crack. They watched as the fissure continued to move up the street like an angry bolt of rocky lightning and then come to a sudden stop.

The kids stared forward at the untouched land at the end of the newly created canyon and gasped. "What….is…..that?" Stacy breathed out in wonder. Her eyes were wide with disbelief.

The ground was changing. It coiled in on itself and pulsed like a living animal, then shot up from the ground into a large, trash-covered mound that seemed to be made of purple flesh and throbbing veins. It grew and swelled like an unwelcome pimple on the face of the earth and reeked with a stench that made the friends' stomachs churn.

A scream sounded out from somewhere behind them and the three kids tore their eyes away from the strange new mass of living earth to the arcade that sat in the parking lot toward their backs. A little girl who appeared to be somewhere around eight to nine years old was darting from the arcade doors with tears streaming down her face. She didn't appear to be aware of the world around her and was running straight toward the creepy, newly formed mountain.

"Don't go that way!" Juicebox yelled at the girl. She stopped her sprint and removed her hands from her eyes to take in the view of the trio, then ran straight into Stacy's arms. Stacy hugged the girl as hysterical sobs were muffled into her jacket.

"What's the matter? Are you hurt?" Stacy placed her hands on the girl's shoulders and pulled her from the embrace to get a good look at her face. "What's your name?"

"Something happened to my brother! In the arcade! The game has him. I don't know what to do," the girl sobbed.

Stacy knelt down so she could look at the girl straight on. "It's okay, take some deep breaths and try to calm down. Tell me what happened, and we will try to help. What's your name?"

"My name is Tessa." The girl sniffed as she wiped her nose with her sleeve.

"Hi Tessa." Stacy smiled at her calmly. "I'm Stacy. This is Juicebox and Jefferson. We really want to help you." Juicebox and Jefferson waved and nodded at the girl encouragingly. "Now what is this about your brother in the arcade? What do you mean the game has him?"

"Henry didn't go to school today. He sometimes skips class to play video games. I knew when I didn't see him at school that he ditched to go to the arcade. I came here looking for him. Things were getting weird everywhere and I was worried." Tessa's already rapid breathing was nearing the verge of full-on panic.

Stacy nodded and placed a reassuring hand on her shoulder. "We know. There is some really weird stuff going on. That must have been super scary for you." Tessa nodded as tears began to flow from her eyes again. "Keep telling us what happened," Juicebox crouched down by Tessa's side as well. "We will figure this out."

"When I got to the arcade it was completely empty and so dark. I walked around looking for Henry and couldn't find him anywhere. Finally, I saw the small glowing light of a screen. Henry was standing in front of it, just staring at the game like a zombie. I tried to get his attention and tell him we needed to go home but he wouldn't look at me! So, I moved myself in front of him to get between him and the game and—" Tessa paused and covered her face with her hands in fear. "When I looked up at him, his eyes were glowing pink! I called his name, but he wouldn't look at me. Then the game started to grow huge and open up, like it had a mouth or something. I jumped out of the way, but Henry just stood there staring at nothing with his pink eyes."

Tessa shook her head vigorously as if trying to shake the image from her mind.

"The game…I can't explain it…It reached out somehow. It pulled Henry inside! It's like the machine melted into him. He's in there right now, tearing the place apart. He tried to get me, too!" It was clear that Tessa couldn't say anything more as she threw herself back into Stacy's arms and sobbed.

Stacy looked up at Juicebox and Jefferson as she held the crying girl. *What do we do?* She mouthed to her friends. Juicebox looked toward the arcade and

Jefferson shook his head. "I know that look, Juicebox."

"We'll save your brother." Juicebox didn't take his eyes from the haunted looking entrance of the arcade.

Jefferson wiped an anxious hand across his face. "We don't know what's going on in there." He placed a hand on Juicebox's shoulder and lowered his voice. "Do you really think it's a good idea to rush in there like superheroes and try to save the day? Look around, man. We might be in way over our heads here…"

Juicebox took one more look at the destruction that surrounded them, and the fleshy mountain that had appeared just moments before. The world was falling apart and he had a responsibility to put it back together. This seemed like as good a place to start as any. On top of that, the pain on Tessa's face tore him up inside. He hated himself for having anything to do with what happened to her brother. He turned and started to walk to the front door of the arcade. "I'm going in. Are you guys with me or not?"

Jefferson let out a breath and hesitantly started following Juicebox. Stacy led Tessa toward a trash can near the entrance of the arcade and urged her to hide behind it. "You stay here, okay? Promise me you won't leave this spot. We will be right back." Tessa nodded and curled her arms tightly around her legs, safely hidden from the view of the street.

¤¤¤

"Plan?" Stacy whispered as she met the boys at the door of the arcade. Juicebox shook his head. "No plan... Let's just try to find this kid and get him out. I don't know what we're going to see in there so let's do our best to stick together." Stacy nodded. Jefferson gulped and looked back toward Tessa hiding behind the trash can. "Maybe I should stay out here with Tessa. To make sure she's okay, you know?" Stacy took Jefferson's head into her hands and manually faced it toward the door. "We need you, buddy. No looking back." Jefferson just sighed and nodded.

Juicebox turned the knob of the door and the three warriors stepped into the darkened entry of the arcade. The place seemed to blink alive a bit as they walked down the first row of broken, glitching games. Eerie neon lights glowed and danced in odd rhythms with every step they took, giving the arcade a strobe-like effect, and sparks flew from half-cut wires and outlets. It was incredible that the place hadn't burned down yet from an electrical fire.

They turned the corner to the next row of games and jumped as overly loud carnival music began to play from overhead speakers. The trio stopped in their tracks and thrust their hands to their ears, searching around for the cause of the unexpected noise. Within a moment, the music cut out, replaced with unhinged bells and dings from the games that whizzed and whirled around them.

The bravery Juicebox had been feeling moments before was beginning to fade. "This place really is freaky." He breathed out. Stacy nodded. "I just keep telling myself it's like the haunted house from the Halloween carnival…" Jefferson rolled his eyes. "The one I refused to go to with you guys?

Fantastic." Stacy pushed him forward. "The point is that if you just keep walking forward, eventually the haunted house ends, and you get to leave without a scratch." A fortune teller machine boomed to life and the face of an old witch sprang forward toward Jefferson. He yelped and clutched at Juicebox and Stacy. "But this isn't a haunted house!" He hissed. "This is real!"

Unsettled, the friends continued their slow march forward, and surveyed every branching pathway as they traveled down aisle after aisle of machines. They didn't see anything that looked like Tessa's brother.

"This place is huge." Juicebox whispered. "I think maybe we should split up." Stacy gave him a nervous look. "If we stay within one aisle of each other, we'll still be close enough to get help if we need it." He reassured his friends. Jefferson pinched his eyes closed in frustration. "Fine… just—everyone stay close by." They agreed and set off down neighboring paths.

Jefferson shook his head as he walked. The day had not been kind to him. First school, then his house and his parents, and now he was roped into yet another monster fiasco for someone he didn't even know. Another machine fired to life as he walked past it, nearly spooking him out of his pants. He rushed to the machine with anger and swung his foot back to kick at it in rage, but something caught the corner of his eye. A soft, calming glow was coming from a game at the end of the aisle. It was a racing game, the kind that had an actual cockpit, seat, and steering wheel with a projected racetrack.

The lights from the game flashed in a mesmerizing pattern, pulling him in like a moth to a flame. There was a woman on the screen, waving a flag. She winked at him and beckoned him forward. Jefferson walked toward the game with curiosity. As he got closer, it was as if the woman had stepped forward and out of the screen. He could see her better and the blood drained from his face as he realized the immenseness of her beauty. She smiled at him widely. "So… beautiful…" He breathed. The woman looked pleased at his choice of words and blew him a kiss. *"Come and play!"* She whispered to him. Jefferson's eyes began to glow in a pinkish hue as he continued to slowly step toward the game.

An explosive crack shot off from somewhere in the back of the arcade and shook the room. As Jefferson stumbled from the rumble, his head cleared, and he was freed from the brief enchantment of the game.

"Juicebox!" Jefferson called out in worry, recognizing that something was playing tricks with his mind. "Juicebox! Stacy! Where are you?" He looked over his shoulder for a split second and saw the video game girl standing there waving her flag inside the screen. He could have sworn she was real just a moment ago.

"Over here!" Juicebox popped his head out from the neighboring aisle, "You okay?" Jefferson shuffled toward his friend without looking back at the game. "What happened?"

"Guys! Come over here!" Stacy called out before Jefferson could answer. The boys ran to Stacy's aisle. "Look there," Stacy pointed to a game sizzling in the corner. "Do you hear those popping noises? It sounds like milk being poured over rice crispies… and see how it's slouched over all weird?"

"Yeah… I think I'm gonna head back outside guys—-" Just as Jefferson began to turn around, the machine sparked and popped, lurching forward like a baby deer trying to stand for the first time. Jefferson ran an anxious hand through his hair. "Like I said, I'm just gonna go outside and make sure Tessa's okay…."

Juicebox moved past Stacy and made his way toward the sound, feeling a surge of that knightly bravery returning to him. Stacy moved forward hesitantly with Juicebox. Jefferson just couldn't make his feet move down the aisle. Another loud pop sounded forcing Jefferson in closer to his friends. As they got closer to the game, they noticed the screen was cracked, and loose wires on the side of the machine shot out occasional fiery sparks.

"What do we do?" Stacy whispered at a loss.

"It's gotta be the machine boy," Jefferson added.

Juicebox slowly reached out his hand to touch the machine. He didn't see any sign of the boy and worried they were there too late to save anyone, including themselves. Everyone's focus was on Juicebox's hand.

The sound of metal scraping against the floor erupted behind the kids from across the aisle. Jefferson jumped and stood facing the side of a giant arcade game with a broken screen. The game box lifted off the ground slowly as it grew spider-like legs. Two metal arms burst through its side with pincers on the ends, ready to attack.

The screen blinked with large letters spelling the words **"GAME OVER."** Behind the screen was the face of the boy looking out with pink glowing eyes. When the eyes settled on Jefferson, the pink glow intensified, and the monster moved into action with precision and speed. Jefferson screamed, turned, and ran past Juicebox and Stacy. He didn't see that they were moving in the opposite direction of where he ran. Juicebox and Stacy ducked behind a heap of broken machines while Jefferson dove behind a pile of boxes and extension cords down the aisle. The monster charged forward with incredible force, throwing machines and crushing everything in its path.

Stacy tried to quiet her hard breathing. The last thing they wanted was for that thing to crash down on them.

"How are we going to beat this one? I'm not so sure we can save the kid."

Juicebox wiped the beads of sweat that were forming on his forehead. "I don't know. But I'm determined to get him out. I need to try and get inside of the game. Did you see where Jefferson ran?"

"Don't these games have doors in the back where they can be repaired if they break?"

Juicebox's eyes brightened. "Yeah, they do! Stacy, you're brilliant!" Juicebox started drawing up plans in his mind as to how he could sneak into the back of the monster.

Stacy looked over at the pile of cords where Jefferson tried to hide. His feet stuck out from behind a box.

"I see Jefferson over there. I have an idea to give you the distraction you might need to get in."

Crouched in his hiding spot, Jefferson put his hands over his ears. A new yet familiar voice had begun whispering to him. He recognized it as the woman's voice from the game.

*"Jefferson? Jefferson? Where are you?"*

Her harmonious chant lilted gently over and over again in his ears. He felt like a sailor being drawn to a siren's song. He tried to resist her words. *"Don't listen, Jefferson,"* he told himself. *"You know it isn't real. There's no way this is real!"* He pinched his eyes closed and tried to control himself.

"Can't …get….it ….out of….my head."

He caved and peeked back at the woman in the game. She beckoned to him sweetly. Suddenly, the room went white in his mind, as if everything disappeared around him. Now it was just him and the game. He stood up and felt light on his feet, as if he was hopping down a hallway made of the fluffiest clouds. Stacy watched as he walked away, knowing something was wrong. Jefferson was smiling widely and stumbling like a drunken fool, and she worried that if she could see his eyes from where she sat, that they just might be pink.

"Change of plans," she told Juicebox. "I need a distraction so I can get to Jefferson now. I think he's in trouble."

"I got you covered," Juicebox responded. He rose and shouted at the boy in the game. "Hey! Over here!" The monster spun around and its screen blinked at Juicebox. A large spark shot from a wire twisting out of the game box as if signaling a thought passing through the boy's mind. In a mechanical fury, its spider legs jolted forward with synchronized precision and rushed toward him.

Juicebox didn't hesitate. He jumped and ran down an aisle away from Stacy. His flashlight bounced a light along the way as he yelled and led the monster across the arcade. He dodged the reaching pincer arms that stretched for him as the monster closed the distance between them. The metallic tapping of the spider-like feet on the tiled floor told Juicebox how close the creature was getting to him. He imagined himself as a hero riding on the wind and pushed his legs to give him superhuman speed forward.

Jefferson didn't seem to notice anything that was happening with the monster or Juicebox. He was completely fixated on the racing game. It called to him. Like an icy cold glass of water on a hot summer day or a big juicy burger after an afternoon of skateboarding. It whispered to him, promising to scratch the itch he couldn't reach.

*"That's right, Jefferson. Come to me and I'll take care of you. I'll make all the bad things go away."* The voice cooed in Jefferson's ear.

Jefferson kept waltzing down his hallway of clouds toward the driver's seat of the game.

*"That's it, Jefferson. Keep walking to me. Let me help you. Let me save you from all the scary things."*

The closer Jefferson got to the game, the wider the opening to the car seat grew, stretching and widening like an angry gaping mouth. Jagged teeth took shape along the opening. By the time Jefferson reached the game, the opened mouth was poised and ready to bite him in half the moment he crossed its threshold.

"You're almost to me, Jefferson. All your pain will be over soon. All anxiety will be washed away. You'll never have to be scared again once you're with me." Jefferson smiled and breathed out releasing the tension in his chest. "Come, sit here in the driver's seat. You will have full control once you take this wheel."

Stacy yelled at Jefferson as she rushed to stop him. All he heard was the sweet sound of the siren's voice.

The mouth opened as wide as Jefferson was tall. *He needed to sit down. The driver's seat offered him control to drive and do what he wanted to do, go where he wanted to go…If he could just sit down.* He started to bend and lift his leg to step into the car.

Stacy flew at him like a linebacker coming in for the last-second tackle.

"No!" She screamed at the game. As soon as Jefferson was on the ground, she jumped up and swung her bat at the game screen. It shattered on contact. Glowing pink shards twinkled into gray and rained harmlessly down onto the ground. A confused Jefferson looked at Stacy with clear eyes. Stacy was looking at the game. Its teeth were curling and melding back into car form. This monster was powerless.

"What happened?" Jefferson got her attention.

"You just about threw yourself into the mouth of a monster, that's what happened!" She wiped a bead of sweat from her forehead. "Like a piece of candy! You were just going to pop right inside!"

Jefferson's eyes widened. Stacy slapped a hand on his shoulder.

"You're welcome for saving your life. Now let's go. We need to help Juicebox." Stacy pointed across the room with her chin. Jefferson saw Juicebox zigzag out of the way of the enormous monster right on his tail.

"We don't have much time. Don't look at any of the screens. We can't tell what is and isn't alive here. Grab that cord and tie it off somewhere across the aisle." Stacy went to the opposite side of the aisle to tie off her end. "Make sure it's tight!"

She jumped up on a game box that was tipped on its side. She looked over and saw that the game had caught up to Juicebox. He was on the ground scrambling away from the pincer arms that threatened to impale him.

She screamed at the monster and beat her bat on the metal below her.

"HEY!!! ELECTRO FREAK!" The monster jerked its gaze toward Stacy. "I've been over here smashing every stupid glowing screen in this sick place! And I'm coming for yours next!" She swung her bat and smashed the screen closest to her. The monster wailed with furious frustration and anger. It immediately seemed to forget about Juicebox pinned to the floor and scurried with intensified speed toward Stacy.

*"Keep coming. We're ready for you,"* she said to herself. Her eyes stared in total concentration at the advancing mechanical beast. Just as the monster reached out to gore Stacy with its pincer hand, it tripped over the outstretched cord and slammed hard onto the ground face down. It slid further down the aisle to a stop as it hit a pile of destroyed games.

Stacy and Jefferson ran to the large pile of debris so that they could jump on the giant monster's back in an attempt to hold it down as Juicebox caught up to them and ripped open the back control panel. The monster groaned and tried to get up. It flailed its arms, feeling around to grab at the kids. Jefferson and Stacy held it down long enough for Juicebox to climb into the back.

"I think there is enough room in here for me to fit," he said as he squeezed through the little door. Once inside, Juicebox saw the boy hanging by wires. Cables were directly attached into the boy's head, several of them pulsing with an energy glow that flowed down the cable from the head to the machine. *"You're using him to power you..."* Juicebox breathed.

He forgot what he was doing in the mesmerizing show of cables and lights. A loud bang broke him from his trance as a pincer hand stabbed through the metal wall of the game and aimed itself directly at Juicebox. He scrambled away from the pincer and glanced out of the cracked screen to see Stacy and Jefferson jumping and yelling to get the monster's attention.

Juicebox started yanking at the cables attached to the boy's head.

"Hey, kid. Can you hear me? I'm gonna get you out of here." A sudden jolt knocked Juicebox to the side as the machine rammed itself into a wall. The boy was unresponsive, caught up in his unbreakable trance through all of the monster's self-destructive rampaging. Juicebox kept tugging at the cables in his head but they wouldn't budge an inch.

"Come on, kid. Wake up!" Juicebox pulled harder at one of the smaller cables attached to the boy. It popped out with a sizzle.

The monster shuddered and for a brief moment, acted as if it was about to shut down. The lights flickered on again, and the mechanical monster started tearing at the outside panels, trying to reach Juicebox. The boy screamed and grabbed at the disconnected cable.

"Must…beat….this….level," he said as he thrashed around.

"Hey, kid! You're not in a game!"

For a split second, the boy's eyes changed from pink to deep blue. He looked at Juicebox, confused. A small trail of blood started to stream down the side of his face where Juicebox had detached the cable.

"Where am I? Who are you?" He tried to turn around, but the small space and cables held him in place. Terror traced the contours of his features.

"That's a loaded question. Right now, we need to get you out of here."

The worried wrinkles on the boy's face relaxed as his trance returned.

"I need to beat this level," His voice was hollow. A claw pierced through the game and missed Juicebox's head by a centimeter. Juicebox moved back away from the boy as much as he could in the cramped compartment.

With Juicebox distracted by the monster stabbing at him, the boy calmly grabbed the snapped cable and tried to reinsert its end into the side of his head.

"I need to beat this level…" he murmured to himself again.

Juicebox reached for the boy's arm, missed at first, then slapped at his hand.

"Kid! This game is out of control!" Juicebox dove to avoid another arm aimed at his head. "The game is hurting you. Try to break free." Juicebox pulled at the biggest cable connected to the boy. "It isn't real! This game is sucking the life out of you!"

"This is all I have," the boy said as he again tried to reattach the cable. "I need to escape, don't you see? THIS is my life now." Juicebox grabbed fiercely at another cable, sweat dripping from his brow as he dodged another attack. "Escape what?!" He cried out. The boy seemed to ponder the question for an annoyingly long period of time. "The boredom? The monotony? The pressure? I don't know. I need to escape all of it!" Juicebox grabbed at the boy's shoulders.

"Trust me, kid. Nothing is boring out in the world right now. Things have changed around here. There's like… monsters and demons running around." The boy cocked a suspicious eyebrow at Juicebox. "Dude! I'm being for real. Take a look around. You've become a freakin' cyborg. Do you remember cyborgs in your regular life?" Juicebox shook the boy's shoulders. "Well… no." The boy looked thoughtful. "Exactly! I'm telling you there's some scary weird stuff out there and I need help fighting it all."

Another pincer burst through the wall of the machine. This time it was aiming for the boy.

"I can tell you more later but we really need to hurry this up. Henry, right? You've got a lot more than this game going for you. And besides that, Tessa is outside waiting for you, and she's scared. We need to get these cables out of your head. Start pulling!"

Juicebox and Henry wrestled with each cable. With each cord they pulled, the monster faltered just a little bit more. Smoke drifted from the circuit board, filling the air with a bitter, acrid, electrical odor. With the last cable out, the spider legs crumbled onto themselves and the entire game crashed into a heap of dusty rubble.

Stacy frantically ran around the pile. "Jefferson, do you see anything?"

"Not yet! Just a heap of dead monster crap!" They dug through the pile of wires and metal monster remains, until they finally reached the debris covering Juicebox and Henry. The boys coughed and wiped at a few bleeding scratches that marked their faces.

"Juicebox, you did it! You killed it!" Jefferson hooted in celebration and offered a hand to both Juicebox and Henry, pulling them out of the metal heap. The remaining lights in the arcade went out, putting an end to the constant buzzing and whirring of the remaining games. The dim light from one solitary window in the room shone through and a refreshing sense of calm fell over the arcade. The evil of the oozing darkness was temporarily gone.

"Let's get out of here," said Stacy in an almost reverent whisper, not wanting to wake up whatever had just gone to sleep.

Walking through the arcade was like walking through the maze of a junkyard in the dimness of twilight. Jefferson followed just a bit behind the others in their trek back to the outside world. He turned to face the game that nearly killed him just one more time. The remaining shards of the screen flicked to life and the faint beautiful glow of the woman beckoned to him.

He pushed the others forward with such force that they all tumbled out of the arcade like synchronized dominoes.

"Henry!" Tessa ran to her brother and threw her arms around his neck. "I thought I would never see the real you again!"

"Tessa! I'm okay. You're choking me," he laughed.

Tears fell down the little girl's cheeks as she clung to her brother. "I was so scared. I couldn't live without you, Henry. Everything is so scary out here now."

"I don't know what happened. I was playing my game and then I was pulled into the machine, and everything went black." Henry explained, then turned to Juicebox. "Now, tell me more about what you said to me in there. I still don't think I really understand what is happening."

Juicebox turned Henry around to face the landscape of what used to be their town. Purple slime dripped from telephone poles, and buildings looked like they had been hit by a hurricane. Pink eyes flickered from the shadows surrounding them, and the grotesque trash covered mountain pulsated as it continued to swell. "Whoa..." Henry breathed in disbelief. "It looks like a freakin' zombie apocalypse out here..." He leaned over to take a better look at some of the goo on the ground.

"Don't touch it!" Stacy warned. "It seems like that stuff has been infecting people and turning them into..." Her voice trailed off.

"Monsters? Like the one I just became?" Henry looked up at her with a wink. She flushed.

Juicebox rolled his eyes and slapped a hand on Henry's back. "You were child's play compared to a lot of what we've seen so far." Henry stood up and smirked. Tessa walked over and grabbed his hand.

Henry looked down at her with a new realization flashing over his expression. "Where's Mom and Dad?" His brows furrowed in concern.

Tessa looked scared. "I don't know. I hope they are at home... A teacher turned into a monster at school today. I was super worried about you but figured you weren't there. I came here looking for you so I haven't even been home yet."

"Monster teacher?" Henry glanced at Juicebox, who confirmed what Tessa said with a quick nod. He looked back at Tessa. "I'm sorry I scared you."

Henry turned back to Juicebox, "Thanks for helping me in there. I think I better go see if everything is okay at home. But I am in for the cause for sure."

He gave a quick fist bump to Juicebox and Jefferson. "I owe you guys one."

Then he turned to Stacy, "And I don't think we were properly introduced. I'm Henry." He took her hand and laid a delicate kiss on her knuckles. "Thank you for saving me." Stacy stared at him with her mouth agape and a cherry-red blush on her cheeks.

Henry put his arm around Tessa. "Let's go home, sis. Not sure what we will find there, but we will face it together." He held his little sister's hand as they walked down the darkening street.

Henry turned around one more time as he and Tessa faded into the dirty pink light of the horizon. "I hope our paths cross again soon!" He waved back as he and Tessa made their way towards their home.

When the two kids were out of earshot, Jefferson gave Stacy a nudge. "Someone was a smitten little kitten…" he said with a sing-song tone.

Stacy looked down at herself. Her clothes were torn and covered in blood and filth.

"Of course, he was. Who wouldn't be over someone like me? I mean, really." She nudged Jefferson back a little harder, then tried to catch him in a grimy hug.

"Hey! Get away," he protested.

Juicebox laughed at his friends, rolling his eyes once more at the thought of Henry's moves on *his* girl. The sky was dark now. He heard the distant screams of victims and the predatorial groans of monsters. He felt like they were being watched from every direction.

Stacy broke the gloomy spell Juicebox was sinking into and pounced on him next. He was caught off guard and clumsily embraced his blue-haired best friend. She settled into the hug and took a deep breath. Juicebox rested his head on hers and they just stood there for a moment in the calm. Jefferson cleared his throat loudly to remind his friends that they weren't there alone. They responded by pulling him into their hug. He resisted at first, trying to wriggle uncomfortably away but eventually surrendered himself to the moment as the three friends took a pause to just breathe.

Stacy pulled away eventually and nudged Juicebox playfully.

"You know, you were a true hero back there," she said.

Juicebox puffed out his chest like a warrior. "I mean... I do what I can..." Jefferson snickered at him but Stacy continued. "You can brush it off if you want. But it's true." She smiled up at Juicebox. He smiled back.

*"HERO?"* The mocking voice poured into Juicebox's mind like a storm. *"SHE DOESN'T KNOW HOW MUCH OF THIS IS TRULY ALL YOUR FAULT... SHE WOULD NEVER SAY THAT IF SHE KNEW THE FULL TRUTH..."*

Juicebox broke his gaze from Stacy's and looked out at the horizon. The voice was right. This whole mess was still somehow his fault. He needed to focus and figure out a way to stop the madness. The weight of his inadequacy for this impossible task crashed down on him again.

He tried to shake the pressure away. "I couldn't have done any of that without you both." He smiled at his friends. "Thank you guys for having my back in there. I—"

The ground suddenly began to shake beneath them and a low rumbling noise echoed through the street. The noise came from the growing pile of rubble and trash. New veins and a webbed looking flesh casing pulsed along the mound with a radical beat. The veins stretched out around it in all directions as if they were searching for something they could suck the life out of.

Jefferson took an instinctive step away from the mountain. "If I were a big scary monster hell-bent on destroying the world with darkness, I would probably set up shop in that trash hill."

"Then that's where we are headed," Juicebox replied. His previously paranoid feelings were now replaced with a wave of anger, urging him to sprint to the growing heap and burn it to the ground.

"*We're coming for you,*" he whispered to himself.

Jefferson looked out into the darkness. A hissing, evil whisper buzzed in his head, but he couldn't understand the words.

"Did you hear something?" He looked nervously from side to side.

"I didn't hear anything. Are you okay?" Juicebox followed Jefferson's gaze and tried to see if something was lurking close by in the shadows. He knew that the darkness was playing with their minds. They needed to be careful. In mere seconds, a taunting whisper could so easily snuff out any hope the friends were trying to cling onto.

Stacy sensed the change in her friends' moods as the sun was going down. Both Jefferson and Juicebox looked worried and unsettled as they stared out into the dark trying to formulate plans.

"The light is fading fast," she said. "We need to find a safer place to camp for the night. It's probably not a good idea to be in the middle of the street next to a monster mountain when the sun goes fully down."

"I agree," Juicebox nodded. The three kids ran in the opposite direction of the growing mountain.

Juicebox looked back and saw a new veiny tentacle grow in the direction of where they had been standing. They would have to wait until the morning to see how the mountain had changed overnight.

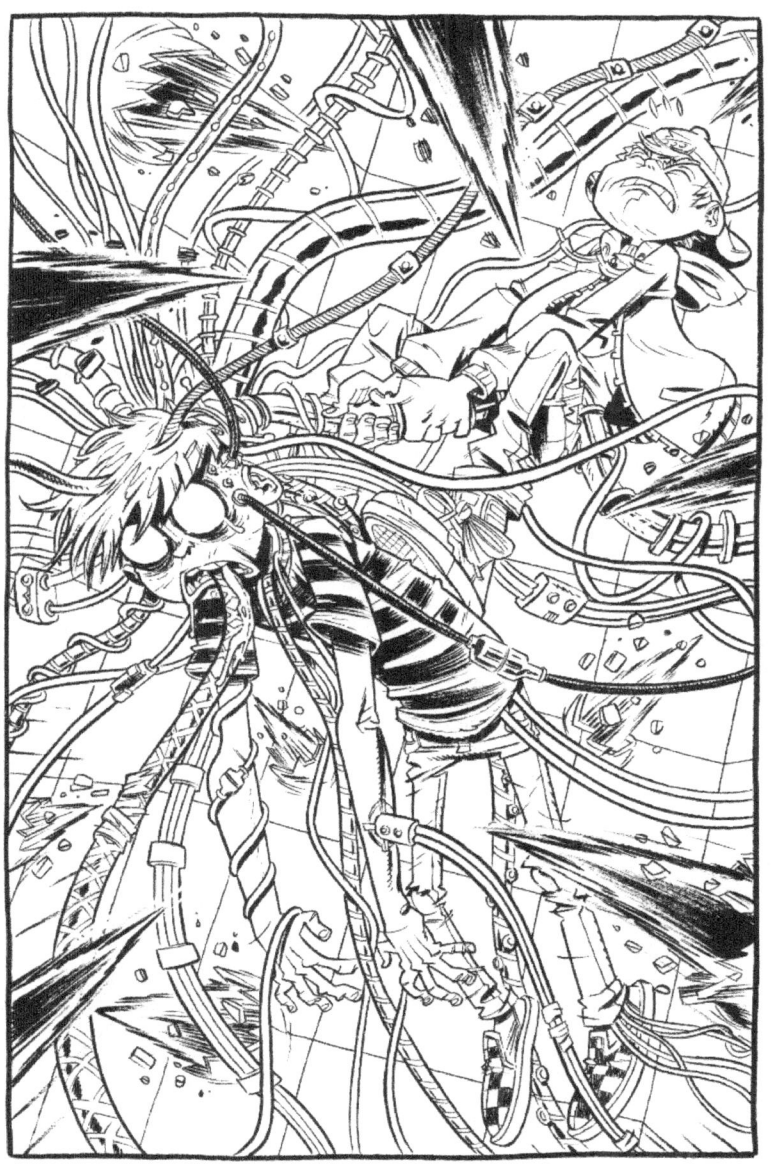

## CHAPTER 11

*"Indeed, the safest road to Hell is the gradual one- the gentle slope, soft underfoot, without sudden turnings, without milestones, without signposts."*

— C.S. Lewis

Juicebox instinctively led his two friends in the direction of the skate park. Not one street in the town was left intact. Buildings and houses stood half-crumbled with piles of garbage littering the sidewalks. Trying to skate down the street was like navigating an obstacle course.

Near the skate park where Juicebox and his friends always felt safe, Jefferson found an oversized, beat-up dumpster that had been tipped on its side at the edge of the park near the main road. The dumpster lid made for a great makeshift door that at least gave the illusion of shutting out the outside world.

As dumpsters went, it was surprisingly clean and it was large enough inside for the friends to set up a comfortable living space. There was even a little hole in the top that acted as a chimney for smoke so that they could build a fire. Stacy laid claim on that task. She was never without her lighter.

"Never know when you might need to start a fire," she always said mischievously, when asked why she carried a lighter when it was a well-known fact that she didn't even smoke.

At least for the moment, with a fire warming up their small new home and the relief of not being chased by hungry demons and creatures, Juicebox felt like he just might get through this current mess alive. He looked at Jefferson on the other side of the fire and at Stacy who was adding more sticks to the flames. He knew there was no way he could kill the darkness without his friends. He couldn't imagine what he would do if this darkness hurt them.

Jefferson looked over at Juicebox and smiled as if the friends were simply out in the woods camping on a relaxing summer evening.

"This is nice," he said and held his hands up to the fire. "Now, who's gonna go find us some hot dogs and marshmallows?"

Juicebox's stomach groaned at the thought of warm food. "I actually grabbed a couple of cans of pork and beans from my Grandma's cupboards. She doesn't cook much, so I'm not sure how old these cans even are."

Jefferson grabbed the cans from Juicebox and held them up with admiration as if they were made of gold. "Beans, glorious beans..." He punched the lids in with a rock and set them near the fire to warm.

Stacy laughed. "I'm going to drink my share down in like one gulp. We need something to go with it so we can have enough strength to fight more tomorrow."

Juicebox peeked outside through a small, rusted hole in their shelter. "We could see if there is anything at the gas station across the street. I sort of see it from here. It looks like there is a light somewhere inside. Most of the store looks dark, though."

Jefferson let out a long-labored breath. "Dude. After the day we just had, you really want to climb back outside into the monster dump for the slim chance at scoring a Twinkie?"

"Ooooh a Twinkie!" Stacy threw the back of her hand to her head and feigned a romantic sigh. "What I wouldn't give for a Twinkie!"

Juicebox looked out the window hole searching for monsters while Jefferson tried to talk sense into Stacy. The street seemed quiet.

"I think we can get to the station and back without any problems. It's just across the street and I'm not seeing anything out of the usual out there." Juicebox turned to look at Jefferson who had his fingers pressed to the bridge of his nose in annoyance.

"You stay here, and me and Stacy will go check out the gas station. I promise — two minutes there, two minutes raiding the snack aisle, then two minutes back."

Stacy squealed in excitement and started rambling on about her favorite potato chips.

"You're gonna get yourselves killed out there." Jefferson shook his head.

Juicebox smirked. "I'm simply in the business of making dreams come true." He glanced at Stacy who laughed and linked her arm through his. Juicebox lifted the door for them both and the two friends headed out into the night just in time to miss Jefferson's last sarcastic remark.

¤¤¤

Main Street seemed deceptively calm. Stacy and Juicebox looked up and down the street several times. Their hearts raced, and they held their breath as they investigated every shadow and possible monster hideout.

"It looks safe. I think we can make it straight to the gas station," Stacy said. They began their mission but were immediately interrupted as Juicebox tripped and banged into a toppled-over metal garbage can in the middle of the sidewalk. The can smacked his knee hard and sent him to the ground, with the noise of his mistake echoing down the street.

Jefferson popped his head out of the opening of the dumpster. Stacy and Juicebox froze in the middle of the sidewalk as the streetlight flicked on directly above them.

"SSHHHH!" Jefferson hissed out at them.

Stacy grabbed Juicebox's arm. "No time for stealth mode. We need to run." Out of the corner of her eye, Stacy thought she saw a large shadow on the building move and turn toward their direction. The soft glow of the fluorescent streetlight made her feel like every monster within a mile of that lamp could now see her and Juicebox standing in the middle of the sidewalk. As much as she hated the new darkness of the town, this spotlight did not give her any comfort.

The automatic door of the convenience store did not open as they expected. Stacy stopped herself before she ran face-first into the glass.

"No!" Juicebox's voice was edgy and desperate. The longer they stood vulnerable on the sidewalk, the more intense his panic grew in his chest. "Help me pry these doors open!" His whisper sounded like a shout in the deadened silence of the street.

"Please, God, make me Superman…" Juicebox prayed out loud as he and Stacy grabbed opposite sides of the front door and pulled. "Truth, justice, and a better tomorrow…" Stacy echoed his prayer through gritted teeth as she leaned back with all her strength.

With a click it cracked open and Juicebox quickly stuck his foot between the doors, ushering Stacy through the opening. He jumped in after her and smacked the doors closed again behind them. Stacy gripped her bat and bumped Juicebox with her hip. "Nice job, Mr. Kent." She whispered. He tipped his backward hat to her, impressed by her own Superman-like strength with the door. "And to you, my dear Kent." They laughed quietly and made their way quickly toward the snack aisle.

They checked out the first row of offerings hoping to find the shelves full of things to eat. The shelves were well stocked with batteries, toothpaste, and various medicines to help with everything from a headache to an ingrown toenail—nothing to eat.

Juicebox turned the corner to inspect the next aisle while Stacy scoped out some of the medicine.

"Jackpot! Stacy, over here," he whispered.

"I'm right behind you," Stacy whispered in his ear. Her unexpected closeness sent Juicebox jumping into the shelves. The metallic wrappers of chips and cookies rattled off pegs. Stacy froze.

"Shoot," she barely whispered.

"Sorry!"

The sound of a single item falling from a shelf on the other side of the store echoed in response to the crashing noise Juicebox had just caused. Then a low growl sounded from the bathroom. The kids did not hesitate to move.

"Grab what you can now and let's go!"

Juicebox followed Stacy's lead. They grabbed everything they could reach and shoved fistfuls of snacks into their backpacks. Another grumble came from the bathroom and the door handle rattled against the lock.

Juicebox shuddered as the evil voice of the darkness began to laugh maniacally in his mind. *"WHAT AN IMPRESSIVE SCREW UP YOU ARE!"*

"I'm so sorry. My fault again," Juicebox said under his breath. The side of his face looked like it was starting to sag slightly.

Stacy huffed and shook her head, still stuffing her pockets. "Nothing is your fault. Pull it together. We need to get out of here. Let's go."

They twisted open the lock of the door and rushed back outside, closing it behind them. Pumping their legs with all the energy they could muster into their tired limbs; they darted back into the dumpster.

Jefferson was laying back, legs crossed with a toothpick between his teeth, enjoying the fire. "Running from monsters I presume?" he asked with his eyes closed.

"Can't…talk…catch…breath…" Juicebox and Stacy were both panting hard from their sprint.

Stacy smacked the toothpick from his hand. "You sure look comfortable!" Jefferson sat up, "Hey! I was using that to pick the beans from my teeth! Juicebox was right, they were old as the hills!"

Stacy glared at him. "You ate without us? Seems like you've been enjoying quite the vacation while we've been gone!"

Jefferson narrowed his eyes at her and held up a finger.

"One—I only ate MY share of the beans. Two—" He held up another finger. "I had to tune into my happy place in order to keep any semblance of sanity while you two were out being reckless for some junk food. Don't you judge me, Johnson." Stacy rolled her eyes and started emptying her pockets.

Juicebox followed suit and the three friends assessed their horde. Jefferson reached for a chocolate bar. Stacy smacked his hand away. "Nuh uh!" She chided him. "The hunters are first to claim their spoils."

Jefferson frowned at her and laid back down. "Fine. But you guys better not leave me with nothing but Funyuns."

Stacy ran a hand through the loot, searching. "Aw man." She sighed. "No Twinkies."

Juicebox shoved a hand into his pocket and pulled out a golden rectangular treat. It twinkled in the firelight. Stacy gasped. "Juicebox I could just kiss you!" He laughed and tossed her the cake. She opened it gingerly and took a bite, groaning with pleasure. Jefferson peeked an eye open and whined at the scene. "Ughhhhh....HEY!–" he yelped as a plastic covered snack cake hit him in the face as well. Juicebox laughed. "Shut up and eat your Twinkie, Jefferson." He sat up and peeled the plastic back, bitterly taking a bite. The sour expression faded from his face as soon as the sugar hit his tongue.

"I'm embarrassed to say that I'll be coming aboard the kissing Juicebox train." He stuffed the rest of the Twinkie into his mouth. They all laughed together, enjoying the warmth of the fire and the sugary treats, finally relaxing a bit from the seemingly never-ending day.

"So?" Jefferson asked after finishing his third bag of chips. "Did you guys see some creepy crawlies in the gas station or were you just running back like hyenas because you were so excited to see me?"

Juicebox's stomach lurched at the memory of the rustling at the bathroom door. He set down his chocolate bar and shook the crumbs from his hands, suddenly not feeling so hungry.

"Something was in the store," Juicebox started to explain. Stacy cut in, "But we escaped *easily*, and locked the door behind us. We should be safe tonight." Jefferson set his food down as well.

"Still, we should keep quiet to make sure nothing finds us... " Juicebox laid back and held his hands to the fire. "In fact, we should probably finish up and get some sleep. Who wants to be the first to keep watch?"

Stacy had just started to suggest that Jefferson take the first watch when a soft knock on the dumpster door turned the three friends to stone. Paralyzed with fear, nobody spoke. The knock sounded again.

Juicebox cleared his throat.

"Um, who's there?"

There was a pause. No one answered. Everyone inside the dumpster held their breath.

A mumbled response finally came through the door, "It's me, Shad. I work the swing shift at the gas station."

Jefferson half-mouthed and half-whispered, "*NO.*" Juicebox shrugged and turned to Stacy. Jefferson insisted, "There is no way we are opening that door! We don't know who that kid is. You just said there was a monster in the bathroom. Remember?!?"

"Does it really matter who the kid is? We can't leave anyone out there alone," Stacy shot back.

"Oh, yes, we can!" said Jefferson. "Don't forget, we have a mission to save the world as we know it! We're planning to march up to that nasty mountain and fix this whole mess tomorrow! The only way that's going to happen is if we protect ourselves first." Jefferson hissed so intently that he spit with every "s" he uttered. Stacy wondered if that effect was intentional. But she understood Jefferson's panic.

Shad softly knocked on the door again. "Hey, I get that you don't know me. And you have no reason to trust me. But is there any way we can talk about this after you let me in? It's really dark out here, and I'm scared. If you don't like me, you can just kick me out."

Juicebox ran through scenarios in his mind. He didn't want to endanger his friends, but not letting in a scared kid seemed like the harshest thing anybody could do. He was determined not to be a monster.

"None of us could survive out there alone." He whispered to Jefferson.

Juicebox sighed and opened the door of the dumpster.

"Hurry, kid. Get in before that thing out there finds us." Juicebox quickly shut the door. "This is Stacy and Jefferson. I'm Juicebox."

Shad looked around at Stacy, Jefferson, and then the pile of junk food on the ground.

"Thanks for letting me in," Shad breathed out in relief. He kept his eyes fixed on the snacks.

Stacy leaned forward and put her hand on his shoulder. "Hey are you hungry? There's plenty here. Have whatever you want."

Shad looked at Stacy with a happy relief and nodded emphatically. "Thank you! I'm starving."

He went to his knees and started to pick out packages to eat. He tore open bag after bag and started scarfing the food as quickly as possible.

"Damn." Jefferson said. "Long shift?"

Shad ignored him and continued tearing apart the snacks. He was shoveling handfuls of food into his mouth.

Juicebox laughed nervously. "We were pretty hungry too. It's been a crazy day out there huh?"

Shad just groaned and chomped. He popped open a can of soda and let it spill messily down his face as he chugged it. He was eating at an unnatural speed. The three friends stared in amazement at the machine-like shoveling motion of Shad's arms.

"Shad, are you okay?" Juicebox stepped over to the boy. Something was wrong but he was at a loss for what to do. He glanced at Stacy. She had a horrified look on her face and backed away from Shad.

"Hey, buddy, slow down there. We have plenty. You don't have to eat so fast," Juicebox said.

Shad looked up and flashed Juicebox a huge, menacing grin. He had food scraps all over his face and one eye started to glow pink.

"Shad! Are you good, man?" Juicebox asked.

Shad kept smiling and then drew in a long, extended breath filling his gut and cheeks with more air than Juicebox thought possible. He looked straight at Juicebox and held his gaze for what felt like an eternity. Without looking away, Shad released a gusty exhale that sent the fire sputtering out. The inside of the dumpster was left in pitch-black darkness.

Stacy screamed.

"Stacy, where are you?!" Jefferson yelled.

Juicebox fumbled for his flashlight. It was clear to him now that he had let the darkness in when he opened the door. He needed light. He needed to save Stacy.

"Jefferson, turn on your flashlight," Juicebox yelled into the darkness.

Flashes of light played off the wall of the dumpster. Every time a flashlight was turned on, a long winding arm smacked it down to the ground. Jefferson managed to click on his light and found Stacy hiding in the back corner of the space and urged her to her feet. They inched their way toward the door as his flashlight was smacked away again, leaving everyone to fight once more in the dark.

Juicebox's eyes darted around in a panic, trying to make out anything he could recognize in front of him. *"ALL YOUR FAULT! YOU'RE WEAK! YOU'RE NOTHING! YOU'RE JUST A WASTE OF SPACE."* Two glowing pink eyes blinked open just in front of his face. He imagined a vicious grin beneath those eyes.

Juicebox couldn't tell if the voice was in his head or if everyone could hear it. But the non-stop physical and mental fighting of the day had left him beyond tired and his hope was dwindling. In the darkness of the dumpster, Shad had shifted into a rubbery beast. His long arms coiled like snakes as they wrapped tightly around Juicebox.

They started to squeeze.

Like an angry, vindictive fist, the monster tightened its grip, squeezing the life out of the boy like juice from a lemon. It was clear that this was a losing battle. If he had learned anything from the day, it was that there was no escaping this darkness that he had brought to life. Juicebox forgot about his friends as he drifted toward unconsciousness.

*"DO YOU SEE NOW THAT MY STRENGTH IS SUPERIOR? THAT THERE IS NOTHING YOU CAN DO TO ESCAPE ME? I WILL ALWAYS FIND YOU. I WILL ALWAYS WIN."*

Jefferson and Stacy pushed the dumpster door open, letting the feeble streetlight send a low glow into the interior of the hideout.

Jefferson saw the monster's arms continue to coil as they closed off at the top of Juicebox's head.

"It's got him!" He screamed.

"I see his foot," Stacy shouted back. "Grab it! We've got to pull him out!"

Stacy and Jefferson grabbed Juicebox's foot, pulling at him like a game of tug-a-war. There was no movement from his leg. No sign that he was conscious and fighting back at the monster. They called out his name.

"JUICEBOX! DON'T GIVE UP!" yelled Jefferson.

"JUICEBOX! DON'T LEAVE US! FIGHT!" Stacy begged.

They pulled together. Tears welled in Stacy's eyes. She let them fall. Jefferson's arms were pulled up into the coil of the creature but he refused to let go. "Flashlight!" He yelled out at Stacy.

Stacy released her grip on Juicebox and fumbled into the dumpster for one of the fallen flashlights. She switched it on and stuffed it up into the arms of the beast where Jefferson was still holding tight to their friend.

The rubbery coil released its grip as if stung by the light as the monster shrieked in pain, stammering backward out the door and into the street. Juicebox and Jefferson followed, carried by the beast's momentum. Jefferson's arms were freed from its grasp, with Juicebox slowly following behind. He lay on the ground staring up at Stacy and Jefferson with pink clouded eyes.

"Juicebox, wake up, snap out of it." Jefferson screamed, shaking Juicebox by the shoulders. "Please, buddy, come back to us." Jefferson felt defeated, wanting nothing more than to just sit and cry with Stacy.

"We need to get him out of the street." Stacy looked down at the gas station. "Jefferson, look." She motioned toward the building. "Do you think we can carry him that far? There is a little bit of light on inside and maybe it will help."

Jefferson nodded. "It's our best bet. Help me lift him up. We might just need to drag him there."

Stacy and Jefferson wrapped their arms across Juicebox's shoulders and half carried him to the gas station. The doors were already open. "It looks like 'Shad,' must have followed us out from here." Stacy mumbled. They scurried through the opening, doing their best to drop Juicebox down as gently as possible, and hurriedly closed and locked the doors.

As Stacy and Jefferson stood behind the glass looking out at the dumpster, a dark shadow slammed into the building, blocking out the glow from the feeble streetlight as it tried to squeeze its long, crooked fingers through the doors. Its shapeless mass seemed infinite. Like a galaxy with no stars. It rammed the glass doors several times before it gave up to chase something else that caught its attention down the street.

Stacy and Jefferson had no words and simply stared out the window, breathless and unsure of what was going to happen next.

Juicebox started to stir on the ground.

"I have the worst headache." He moved up onto his elbows and rubbed at his temples.

Stacy fell to the floor and embraced him, tears running down her dirty face. "I'm so glad you're okay. I thought we really lost you."

The last thing Juicebox remembered was giving up all hope against the darkness that surrounded him.

Jefferson bent down and patted him on the knee. "You scared us bad out there."

His friends were visibly shaken. He felt terrible for scaring them so badly. He also just felt terrible in general. "I'm so sorry you guys. I let that monster in. I made a bad call. Again."

Stacy shook her head. "Shad was very convincing, Juice. I would have done the same thing." She squeezed his hand. The sight of her tear-stained face filled him with agony.

"I mean... I wouldn't have..." Jefferson started. Stacy snapped at him. "Not because you knew it was the darkness!" Jefferson cowered a little.

"You would have denied Shad out of fear. You didn't know what he was, any better than Juicebox did."

Jefferson shrugged. Juicebox tried to sit up a bit more. "Fear has a purpose though, doesn't it?" He tried softening Stacy's blow to his friend. "Fear is what keeps us alive in a way. It's only the fear of being hit by a car that keeps you from running into the middle of the street. It's the fear of dying that keeps you from eating rat poisoning. Fear isn't always a bad thing. It has its job and its place. I think sometimes our fears can be our protection."

Stacy looked down the aisle, thoughtful.

"Maybe that's my problem. I've got plenty of fears. But I'm not so sure they're ever wearing the right uniforms."

Jefferson scratched his head and Stacy continued to think on Juicebox's words.

Juicebox looked out the glass doors and glanced at the monster mountain in the distance. It had grown and was surrounded by various fires that burned across town. The reflection of their tiny glowing lights twinkled in his eyes against the darkness of the room.

"Someone toss me that bag of marshmallows." Jefferson flung the puffy bag to his friend. Juicebox laid his head down onto it and closed his eyes.

"We need to get some sleep."

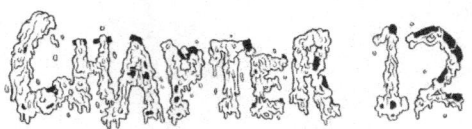

*"I am all in a sea of wonders.
I doubt; I fear; I think strange things which I dare not confess to my own soul."*
– Bram Stoker

The morning dawned in shades of polluted pink and purple casting an ominous haze across the town. "I always hated pink." Stacy grumbled at the distorted color of the sky as they washed their faces with water bottles outside the gas station. "What ever happened to blue? I miss blue!" She spread her arms out, motioning all around them. "There is literally none to be found!"

Juicebox gave her a tired smile. "There's still a quite striking shade of blue from where I'm standing." Stacy stared at him confused. Jefferson rolled his eyes. Juicebox took off his hat and threw it to Stacy. "Here, cover it up. It's distracting me." He poured a water bottle through his dirty blonde hair. Stacy stared at the hat confused, until realization flashed across her face, causing her to blush.

Jefferson snickered. "And I see a new shade of pink. Just…. there." He poked at Stacy's cheek. She punched him hard in the arm.

The gang began their walk, each feeling tired and uneasy, on the lookout for the next new boogeyman of the day. Stacy hated the sound her boots made as she walked across the littered street. Broken glass and garbage crunched under each step sending echoes down the road. She usually loved to break things. Always on the hunt for a glass bottle to throw at a wall while she was out skating in the streets. But today, in this moment, Stacy longed for softness. She ached for things to be put back together, rather than broken apart.

"Hey! Look at that!" Jefferson pointed to a building off to their right. His voice was barely above a whisper.

Stacy and Juicebox looked to the side and saw the building Jefferson pointed to. It was morphing into something that barely resembled the apartment complex it used to be. Fleshy veins grew up on the outside walls and pulsed as if they were connected to a massive heart somewhere deep within the innards of the structure. Small veins branched off the larger ones and covered the building in a network of grotesque living tissue.

"What do you think it is?" Stacy asked.

"It looks like the sickness has now spread to the buildings," Juicebox replied. A wave of guilt passed through him, sending a visible shiver down his spine. He couldn't take his eyes off the decaying building and wondered how fast the town was changing. How quickly would the town be consumed by the infection of this monster? He stared at the veiny walls as he walked past. Hearing the pulsing beats and gurgling groans from the now living structure, not paying attention to what was in front of him.

"Watch out!" Stacy yelled as the pavement in front of them began to crack and break open. A huge sinkhole appeared across their path in the road. She instinctively grabbed Juicebox's shoulders in time to stop him from taking his next step and falling in. The three friends very carefully walked up to the edge to investigate the opening. The hole revealed a purple river flowing underneath the road. Juicebox, captivated by what he was seeing, leaned in too far and almost lost his footing. Stacy grabbed his arm and tore him away from the edge.

"Stacy saves the day," Jefferson clapped both of his friends on the back.

Stacy flicked her hair back like a runway model. "It's what I do." She smiled at Juicebox but he wasn't looking at her. His shoulders were slumped and his eyes were baggy and red. The weight of his guilt, the constant near death encounters… it was just way too much and it was showing very clearly on his body and his face. Stacy shot a questioning look at Jefferson. He shrugged, not knowing what to say. The chaos surrounding them was getting tedious for everyone. They all stared down again at the river.

"I can't believe the road could just split open like that. Did you see how deep that hole is? A semi-truck could get lost down there. I wonder how many rivers of that nasty stuff are tunneling under the town?"

Juicebox wasn't listening to the chatter from his friends. The darkness was swimming again through his mind. *"YOU COULD JUST JUMP IN AND END THIS ALL RIGHT NOW,"* the darkness whispered. *"WHAT'S REALLY THE USE ANYWAY? YOU KNOW DEEP DOWN THERE'S NO FIXING THIS."*

Jefferson looked over at Juicebox as Stacy asked her question. He saw a tear roll down Juicebox's face, eyes fixed on the dark river swirling and bubbling below him. Jefferson thought it looked as if Juicebox was slowly leaning toward the edge of the gap in the street.

"Juice. Back up. I know it's a lot right now but we are figuring it out together. Back away from the edge."

Something in Juicebox snapped and darkness filled his mind with a rage he had rarely felt before. Jefferson's words weren't a friendly reassurance but an almost unbearable annoyance that was now the source of his anger.

He shoved Jefferson away from him. "Even if by some miracle we defeat this monster," he snapped back, "nothing will change! I still am who I am, a stupid, selfish kid that causes nothing but trouble and hurt to everyone! I can't bring my parents back. I can't tell them that I'm sorry! And I can't change any of this terrible mess that I've caused!" He shook with anger and his face sagged slightly. He snarled as his lips pulled back to show his teeth. Jefferson took a defensive step away from Juicebox.

Juicebox saw true fear flash across Jefferson's face. He looked down at his hands which were balled up into white knuckled fists. He relaxed them and forced himself to slow his breathing, shaking his head at himself. Had he really just pushed and yelled at his best friend? Whatever hold the darkness had on him was not going to cross that line. He took a deep breath and shook his head.

"Jefferson, I'm so sorry. I don't know where that came from. I didn't even really hear you. There was this voice in my mind telling me to jump and I guess my anger just took over." He looked up at

Jefferson, "I didn't mean anything I said. I almost lost it there. Things are just getting to me, you know?"

Jefferson nodded and motioned to the purple goo covering the ground below them. "It's this stuff. It's getting to all of us! I feel it too. You're not alone, Juicebox."

Jefferson nudged Juicebox's arm. "Just don't push me again. I've got some moves and I'd hate to have to use them on you." He managed to get a slight smile from Juicebox right as the ground began to rumble and shake beneath them once more.

The three friends darted away toward the building, trying to escape the scene as the sinkhole stretched open wider. Large chunks of pavement crumbled and smashed into the thick, purple slime below.

The team pressed forward and a deep groaning noise filled the air as another rumble shook the town sending more buildings to the ground. Car alarms beeped and blared, and a deep alarm horn sounded, drawing their attention down Main Street as far as they could see.

The strange, living hill that peeked up from the ground the day before was sprouting upward at terrible speed, becoming an enormous mountain that quickly towered higher and higher. Its growth caused destruction to everything surrounding it. Cars flew up into the air as if they were toys, and trees toppled over like dominoes. The oozing river seemed to flow faster and ripped through yards and sidewalks to change its course toward the mountain, feeding it, like veins rushing blood to a beating heart.

It's one thing to watch a scene like this from a movie, snuggled up on your couch with popcorn and a blanket—enjoying the entertainment of artificial destruction. It's another to see something like this on the news. The reality of the terror might hit you just a bit more—but still, you're on your couch. Not out in the hurricane or war zone you just watched on channel three. You can shut your eyes. You can turn it off. You can lock your door and go to sleep and forget about it with a small prayer that someone else will help those poor people you saw suffering on your screen. And then you can wake up the next day without giving it a second thought.

It is something else entirely to watch this level of destruction with your own eyes. It's the stuff of nightmares to witness disaster so personally. There is no separating yourself to spare your peace of mind. Closing your eyes doesn't stop a tree from falling and crushing you to bits. There is no off button on the remote of reality to stop a bomb from going off. So, the scene that played in front of the three friends' eyes was not just scary. It was bone chilling. It was life changing. And the terror they felt was paralyzing.

Juicebox was the first to speak and try to break the spell of horror they had been put under. "We need to pick up the pace and get to this mountain. If we don't hurry, soon there will be nothing left to save. We have to keep going."

He took a confident step forward toward the mountain, when a piercing pain stopped him in his tracks. "AAHH!" He doubled over, the color of his face distorting into muddy shades of blue as if he were choking. His eyes, veiny and red, bulged outward like a bullfrog. He fell to his hands and knees, quivering as he tried to breathe through the pain.

"Let me get you some water!" Stacy's fingers fumbled with the zipper of her backpack as she searched for a water bottle and handed it to him shakily. Juicebox swatted at the bottle, sending it flying through the air. "Get away from me!" Juicebox's voice was distorted and didn't sound like his own. Stacy scowled at him and backed up. She and Jefferson watched from a distance until Juicebox was able to regain his footing. He resumed his walk with shaky steps forward, his friends following just a bit behind.

They sidestepped over the sidewalk and continued down the road, avoiding fallen building walls and knocked-down utility poles. Every block they walked felt like a mile. Still, the fleshy mountain in front of them slowly grew closer.

They passed by the remains of the local carwash. The billboard seemed to have survived the wreckage. Juicebox glanced up at it expecting to see the familiar view of a cartoon bubble washing a shiny, red truck. Instead, he saw glowing pink eyes and a menacing smile with razor sharp teeth. The monster glared at Juicebox with the caption reading,

## "I WILL ALWAYS BE THERE!"

"I'm not feeling so good," he said.

Jefferson noticed the sign as well. "Me either."

Stacy spotted a bench in the alley next to the carwash, hidden just a bit from view. "Do you guys need to sit down for just a second? There's a bench that's pretty well hidden from sight. Maybe we should take a quick rest."

Juicebox shook his head. "We really need to keep going. We're moving at the speed of slugs."

Jefferson looked at the bench with longing, then glanced back up at the billboard. The monster's eyes blinked at him. He shuddered.

"Juicebox is right. Let's keep going."

A small cry echoed from the alley near the bench. Jefferson threw his hands up. "Of course."

"Maybe it's another kid down there who needs help," replied Juicebox. "Should we go look?" He glanced at Stacy hoping she would weigh in on what they should do. He didn't trust his judgment right now. The last thing they needed was a repeat of Shad. They heard the crying again. Whoever was making the noise sounded like they were really upset.

Juicebox wiped a hand down his face and started walking toward the sounds. "Let's go help whoever it is. That's the right thing to do no matter the outcome."

Jefferson nodded. "We just better have a good plan before I step into those shadows."

Stacy twirled her bat. "Not much we can really plan for except swinging at any monsters that come our way. Go grab something to fight with, and we'll be on guard. I think that's all we can really do at this point."

Jefferson grabbed a broken piece of pipe from a fallen street sign he found on the sidewalk and Juicebox clutched his skateboard with the wheels and trucks facing outward.

Into the alley they went with weapons in hand. The air in the shadows felt cool, but somehow unwelcoming. They could hear the whimpers coming from further down the way.

"Hello down there? Is everything okay? Do you need any help?" Stacy called out in a whisper-like tone as they very slowly moved down the alleyway.

No one could see very far down, the deeper in they got the darker it got as well.

A loud crash sounded sending Jefferson bolting backward and Stacy, in a panic, began to swing her bat frantically. A mutated cat sat on the edge of the dumpster, cleaning itself, beside them. It had knocked down a pile of garbage. It scurried away at the sight of Stacy's bat. "It was just a cat!" Jefferson breathed clutching at his heart.

The cries started again. Stacy called out to the hidden stranger, "Hello? Can you hear me?" She lifted garbage bags and metal scraps searching for the source of the whimpers. The crying stopped and an uncomfortable silence followed. Each friend tried to find something to fix their eyes on in the darkness of the alley. They were all ready to bolt back to the street if a monster came attacking. A rotten apple whizzed past Juicebox's head as a low guttural noise heaved in the dark.

"Go away!" a girl yelled at them. Another piece of fruit hurled towards Jefferson, but he shuffled to the side before he got a mouthful of the rotten mess.

"Go away!" they heard again. "Don't look at me! I don't want anyone to see me like this!"

Juicebox looked at Stacy with one eyebrow raised. "What does that mean?" Stacy shrugged her shoulders.

"Don't be afraid," Stacy replied back down the alley. "We are here to help you!" They took a few more steps down the middle of the alleyway. Jefferson and Juicebox stayed close to Stacy's back. They kept checking behind themselves, half-expecting something with pink eyes and purple ooze to jump on them from one direction or the other.

They finally came to the crying figure. The three friends held back a bit, trying to focus their eyes on what exactly they were looking at. This thing almost looked like a girl, but its back was distorted and lumpy. The entire creature looked out of proportion, stretched out, and bloated. Where the skin was stretched too far, Juicebox thought he could see a seam that was splitting around both sides of the body.

The seam was tight and bursting with holes making her skin look like it could tear away from her body at any moment. Juicebox noticed that the small holes which were torn along the girl's skin showed patches of blue and sticky, matted fur.

Jefferson was the one who noticed the girl's normal-looking hair, two pigtails tied up on both sides of her head. "Wait a minute! We know this girl! Isn't that Meredith from math class? Look at her pigtails. I've sat behind those tails all semester."

"You mean Mere-Death?" Juicebox whispered back. "I think you're right. I haven't seen her much this year."

"Maybe that's because you haven't been to math class much this year," Jefferson teased.

The changing girl heard the boys talking about her and jumped up, enraged. "Don't call me that!" She stood up and turned to the three friends. They looked at her with wide unbelieving eyes. Jefferson sucked in his breath and took a step back.

"What is that?" his whispered question was barely audible.

Meredith threw her arms around, knocking her knuckles against a fire escape ladder that scaled the wall to the roof. The pipe on the side of the ladder buckled as if it were made of cardboard. Her bulging and bloated body towered over her classmates. Stacy and Juicebox backed up as well. They were all ready to dart away from Meredith the monster, but Meredith the girl was still there too.

She started to cry again. "Please help me. I don't know what to do." She sat back down on the ground, rolled almost into a ball, and cried. The curve of her back and the slump of her shoulders showed the quivering seams that followed from under her clothes that looked ready to split open at any moment. Small tears in these seams showed wiry blue fur that started to poke through, along with purple ooze seeping out like goopy blood coming from a wound.

Jefferson looked at the girl. He couldn't hide his disgust. "Meredith, what's happening to you?" He didn't want to see what the girl would look like if her skin burst open and sluffed off her body.

"I don't know!" She wailed. Stacy stepped forward reassuringly. "Let's just back up, why don't you try explaining the last thing you remember before this happened to you."

Big wet tears rushed like a river down Meredith's face. "I was feeling good about myself today. For once! I actually felt some sort of confidence. I got this new makeup to wear to school to hide…" Her voice drifted off.

"The pimples?" Jefferson suggested. Meredith growled at him. "YES. THE PIMPLES." Jefferson backed up and fell against a trash bag that was propped up behind him. Meredith moaned. "Anyway, it worked really well. And I was feeling pretty good. I got all dressed up in my favorite outfit and set out for the day thinking that just maybe, nobody would comment on my stupid ugly face." She hid her face in her hands and cried.

"But of course, Jeremiah Rogers couldn't let me have one day of peace. One day of being just a normal girl at a normal school. He walked up to me in the hall in front of everyone before the bell and called me a cake face. 'Did you think all that frosting was going to hide the messed-up cake underneath?' He taunted me and everyone laughed. It was HUMILIATING. So, I ran into the bathroom and scrubbed it all off in the sink and just cried staring at my ugly reflection. But then I noticed this weird purple drip coming from the ceiling above me and I looked up just as it fell and hit me square in the nose. Suddenly I was morphing into this…. THING. I've become some sort of MONSTER."

Meredith groaned as her skin stretched. Her physical discomfort seemed directly linked to her emotional pain. "Now my skin really hurts. I just hurt all over! I feel like I could burst at any moment!" She began to scream in pain and pull at her face, stretching it out and almost tearing it off.

Stacy took a step towards Meredith.

"Meredith, I don't think you're a monster," Stacy started. "We can help you. I feel like there is more we should try to talk through…"

"I've been asking for help for years! Nobody ever helps!" Meredith started to cry again, her skin bulging and tearing the more her tears fell.

Stacy crouched down to her level; it was clear to her that Meredith's emotional distress was triggering the physical changes. "I'm so sorry that you haven't gotten the help you needed. Let me try to help you now."

"You?! Help me?!" Meredith started to raise her voice. Her back was still to Stacy, but she started to twist around to look at her. "Have you ever even noticed me? Have you ever really even seen me? NO!!!!" Meredith stood up in front of Stacy with glaring pink eyes. "No one ever noticed!" She reached her hand up to her face. The skin of her hand burst along the seams between her fingers and her newly clawed fingertips scraped down the skin of her cheek. Bloody purple liquid ran down her face and pooled on the cracked, uneven concrete below.

"I don't blame you for not seeing me. I wish I could stop noticing myself. I don't want to see my awkwardness, my ugliness, my, my... monsterness! But the bullies see it. They hate me. And no one wants to be my friend. People either don't notice me at all or they notice me too much. And it makes me constantly uncomfortable in my own skin. I hate my skin! AAAAHHH! IT HURTS!"

Meredith twisted in pain. She scratched and pulled at her skin, first wrapping her arms around herself and tearing at her back with them. The seams swelled and tore revealing mangy, matted fur beneath.

"Something is happening! AAAAHHHH!" Meredith continued to squirm in discomfort and panic. "It hurts so bad! Why won't someone help me?!?" She screamed.

Juicebox stepped forward next to Stacy. "It's okay, Meredith. Really. Try to calm down. Your panic is making it worse!"

"Ahhh!" Meredith screamed.

Her skin was bubbling with huge growing blisters all over her body. Her clothes were stretched and ripped as she grew larger, towering over them more and more. The seams on her arms and neck were bulging to their bursting point.

Meredith continued to scream. "I just want to disappear!"

Juicebox stepped even closer to her. "Meredith, listen! I think this is just in your head. Try thinking about something good. Listen to my voice. Fight this thing! We can help you figure this out!"

"IN MY HEAD?!? Is that what you think?" She spun around to face Juicebox, and popping noises went off like buttons snapping loose from their threads. POP, POP, POP. The seams that ran along Meredith's face, neck, arms, and legs burst open. Pieces of her skin fell off in gory chunks or hung off her body from thin strands of bloody tissue.

Juicebox instantly recoiled from the wafting stench of rotting flesh that came from Meredith. She raged and raked her clawed fingers down her face.

The plain girl that hardly anyone noticed at school, had disappeared. A pigtail bow slowly fluttered to the ground and landed next to Juicebox's foot. In the girl's place stood a nine-foot-tall monster. She uncurled her slumped back and stood to her full height. Pink glowing eyes darted from Juicebox to Stacy, then to Jefferson who made a face and raised his arm to shield his mouth and nose from the stench with the crook of his elbow.

Stacy looked at the monster's skin with patches of scabby bumps and tufts of blue fur. She saw the strange purple drips seeping out of wounds where Meredith had torn off her own skin. There was nothing about the monster that resembled the girl.

"Meredith? Can you still hear me?" She hesitantly asked.

The monster focused on Stacy. Her beady glowing eyes were unsettling. She hunched down slightly, ready to lunge, and let out a menacing shout.

*"AAHHHHHH!"* came her demonic scream. Her open mouth showed flat hammer-shaped teeth that could grind and mash a person to smithereens. *"IT... DOESN'T..... HURT.... ANYMORE! BUT YOU WILL!"*

"Uhm... guys... " breathed Juicebox.

"Run!" Jefferson shouted, bolting down the alleyway.

The Meredith monster bounded after the kids with explosive strength. Small flaps of skin clung to her limbs as she ran. Juicebox slipped in a puddle of filthy water at the mouth of the alley and fell face down on the ground. The monster, unable to stop her momentum, flew over Juicebox, her foot missing his head by less than an inch. She yelled and growled and slammed into a car, breaking all of the windows. The impact of the crash lodged her into the frame of the car, which she struggled to escape from.

"I'm heading there," Jefferson pointed to a large farmhouse on the top of a nearby hill with a giant iron gate blocking a dirt driveway. Juicebox quickly pushed himself up and ran past where the monster was smashing at the car as if it were a ball of tinfoil. Stacy was running fast just behind Jefferson. She looked back at Juicebox.

"Hurry!" she encouraged. "She won't be stuck for long." Juicebox moved as fast as he could to catch up with his friends. They all raced in the direction of the house, making it halfway up the hill before the monster freed herself from the mutilated car.

"*AAAAHHHHHH!*" she screamed in angry obsession—racing toward the hill.

Jefferson danced around the gate and rushed to the door, banging his fists loudly on the wood. "I don't think anyone is here!"

He knocked louder. "Hello! Is anyone there? Please open the door!"

Nobody was answering. "We don't have much time."

"I'm not sure this door will even keep Meredith out," Stacy added.

"That's not Meredith," Juicebox said. He looked in through the window knocking over the wicker rocker on the porch. "I can't see anyone. Just try opening the door."

Stacy jumped at the sound of the loud guttural growl from the monster raging up the hill quickly closing in on them and danced in place anxiously. She turned the knob, and the door swung open. Without any need for encouragement, all three kids rushed into the house.

Jefferson slammed the door behind them. They fell to the floor and scampered to hide themselves against a nearby wall. Even with their labored breathing, they tried to be as quiet as possible. Juicebox tilted his head to listen for any sounds of the approaching beast.

The sound of claws scratching along the pickup truck parked out front rang painfully through their ears, quickly followed by the heavy thump of the monster's feet on the front porch step.

"The front door!" Jefferson hissed. "It's not locked!"

Stacy dove for the door and twisted the deadbolt seconds before the doorknob started rattling.

**BANG, BANG!**

Stacy was jolted forward as Meredith began ramming herself against the door trying to get in. She roared in frustration. Silence followed her screams. Juicebox, Stacy, and Jefferson looked at each other and waited through minutes that felt like hours in the quiet.

"Is she gone?" whispered Jefferson. Stacy rolled to her knees to peek out the window.

"I don't see anything," she quietly reported. A thunderous growl echoed from the side of the house.

"Oh shoot!" Stacy slammed back down against the wall.

"What?" Jefferson's tone was panicked.

"She saw me!"

Glass crashed into the room as Meredith dove into the window head-first in a fit of madness. The three kids sprang to their feet, each grabbing at anything that could be a possible weapon against the beast. They stood arched and ready for the impending battle.

An eerie screech blared in the distance from the center of town, chilling each of them to the bone. Somehow the distant call sounded more menacing than even Meredith's creepy low growls. They looked out the window beyond the monster and felt a sinking sense of despair at the call.

Meredith immediately stopped her struggle through the window. Her monstrous head tilted to one side as if listening to something commanding. She let out a primal groan of painful disappointment and glared at the kids as she pulled her body back through the jagged glass-laced hole. The intent stare of her eyes sent the message that this fight was not over.

When the Meredith monster was gone, the sharp shards of the window's glass dripped with her purple blood. It pooled on the floor signaling that the beast received some significant damage in her efforts to chase the three friends.

"Is she gone?" asked Jefferson. "I'm too scared to look." He was shielding his eyes, still clutching at the lamp he had grabbed to fight the monster a moment before.

"Something's out there," said Juicebox. He and Stacy still stood in their fighting stances, not yet ready to relax even though the room was silent. They didn't hear anything inside or outside of the house. Stacy took a few careful steps toward the gaping window hole.

"I don't see anything. I think it, or Meredith, or whatever she is now, is gone." She sat down on the couch with a heavy sigh. "I wish we could have saved her." Sadness flooded her face as she ran a tired hand through her electric blue hair. Juicebox and Jefferson followed her to the couch. Jefferson tried to cheer her up. "There's still time. We've got to keep the hope that all the monsters out there can be changed back to normal. That's why we've got to get to that mountain." He thought of his parents in their monster form and felt a renewed resolve to find a solution to their problem as quickly as possible.

"I know." Stacy breathed. "It's just so hard to watch the darkness spread so intensely like that." She thought of Meredith's scared face, the pain in her eyes before she completely transformed into the monster she so desperately wanted to escape. She laid her bat down on the ground, feeling like a candle snuffed out by the wind.

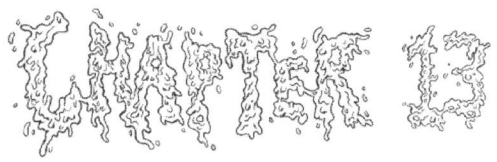

*"I became insane, with long intervals of horrible sanity."*
*- Edgar Allan Poe*

Juicebox rested his head on the arm of the couch, letting his thoughts drift. It felt like every few steps they took forward were immediately followed by three steps back. Reaching the mountain should be the easiest part. All they had to do was walk there. But every step of the way was filled with problems and roadblocks. The road splitting open beneath them, kids needing help then morphing into monsters, ooze falling from the sky threatening to infect them… the simple walk to the mountain had become nearly impossible. And then there was the question of what they would even do once they got there.

His friends were chatting, but Juicebox had all but tuned them out. He opened his tired eyes, noticing the afternoon sunlight streaming in across the woven rug in front of him, making patterns of lines that stretched from one side of the room to the other. In the sideways light, he noticed tiny dust motes calmly floating in the air. The motes were strangely peaceful after the violent action that stirred them up in the first place.

His eyes drifted from the dusty light to the shadows lurking in the corner of the room. He stared into the darkness mindlessly. It was odd. Everything the shadows touched seemed to shift and warp as if they were placed in front of a funhouse mirror. The sound of his friends' voices faded more and more the longer he stared.

¤¤¤

The room began to fade to gray as all colors started melting from the walls. Juicebox instantly snapped to alert and sat up on the couch as the shadows in the corner of the room gathered and combined into a large cloudy mass, as dark and deep as a starless midnight sky. The shadow's presence was cold, and Juicebox felt his breathing hitch with fear. He wrapped his arms around himself for warmth. He couldn't seem to move or speak or look away from the vastness of the shadow.

Two large pink glowing eyes opened in the dark.

*"HELLO, JUICEBOX,"* said a smooth but mocking voice. *"I SEE THAT YOU'RE ALONE... AGAIN."* It said with a chuckle.

Juicebox's vocal cords were still paralyzed. He tried to turn his neck to search for Stacy and Jefferson but could not move an inch. His eyes, however, were clearly able to see that the couch beneath him was empty, the entire room now flooded with the darkness. He flicked his eyes back to the shadow.

*"LIKE I SAID, YOU'RE ALONE. BUT DON'T WORRY. YOU'VE GOT ME FOR COMPANY."* The darkness laughed wickedly. *"AND I CAN ASSURE YOU, I'M NOT GOING ANYWHERE."*

Juicebox tried to make his legs move. He needed to get out of here. He needed to run. His foot squeaked half a centimeter forward then glued itself in place once more. His teeth gritted, pressed tightly together as he tried to yell out for help to no avail.

*"DO YOU UNDERSTAND NOW? YOU WILL ALWAYS BE...ALONE."* Low chuckles grew into the vibrating staccato of a devilish cackle.

The laughter stopped as the touch of a cold hand grasped his shoulder and he felt a low sigh directly in his ear. *"ALONE."* The voice whispered. Juicebox tried to thrash away. *"ALONE!"* The grip on his shoulder tightened. The voice seemed to have entered directly into his mind now and echoed it's song repeatedly within the walls of his skull. *"ALONE. ALONE! ALOOOONE. ALONE!!!!"* The voice bellowed and roared. Juicebox continued to try thrashing away. He felt the cold, hard hands of the darkness pressing down on his chest, taking away his ability to breathe. He gasped, willing his lungs to be filled with air. The hands moved to his mouth, nearly cutting off his breathing completely.

Juicebox rampaged through the hallways of his mind, tearing apart files, toppling over boxes to locate some idea of how to fight this thing. The word came to him. *Light.* Light was what had sent the darkness out before. But standing here, paralyzed in this darkened room, how was he possibly going to get it?

He stopped struggling against the cold pressing of the darkness and closed his eyes to the shadows that covered him, channeling all of his energy into the recesses of his mind to bring an image to its forefront. *Just picture it.* He told himself. *Picture a soft, pleasant, glowing light.*

He brought the image forward and focused on it. The little glowing ball was small. Just the flicker of a flame. But it lightened his mind. "I see it." He said out loud. The darkness released its grip on his chest. *"YOU SEE NOTHING."* It replied. *"ALL THAT IS HERE IS ME. ALL THAT IS HERE IS DARKNESS."*

Juicebox ignored its words and continued focusing on the little ball of light in his mind. It grew brighter as he stared at it. He felt movement return to his hands and feet.

*"OPEN YOUR EYES. I'LL SHOW YOU ALL THERE IS TO SEE."* He continued to ignore its words. The darkness laughed. *"IF YOU THINK YOU CAN HIDE INSIDE YOUR MIND YOU ARE SORELY MISTAKEN. I LIVE THERE TOO, REMEMBER? NOW LET ME SHOW YOU WHAT I MEAN."*

Suddenly, images began to flow behind his eyelids. He saw his mother wiping a tear from her face as they drove down the road on that fateful day. The worst day of his life. He saw his dad, with rage behind his eyes as he turned back to face him in the car, asking him to apologize. He saw the crash and the ambulance. The purple ooze falling from the sky. Mrs. Gill nearly biting Stacy's head off, and Jefferson's parents transformed into monsters.

Juicebox tore his eyelids open to escape the scene of memories.

*"DON'T YOU SEE? THIS IS WHAT IS REAL. ALL THE PAIN THAT YOU HAVE CAUSED. ALL THE DESTRUCTION THAT YOU HAVE CREATED. THIS IS WHY YOU ARE ALONE. THIS IS WHY YOU WILL ALWAYS BE ALONE."*

Juicebox glared into the glowing eyes of the beast. "NO!" He screamed out. "This is your fault. It's not mine. I never wanted this! I never set out trying to create any of this! It was always you!"

The darkness rushed forward at him, its pink eyes blinking chaotically in his face. *"TELL THAT TO THE PARENTS YOU KILLED! TELL THEM HOW IT WASN'T YOUR FAULT THAT THEY DIED."*

Tears started to gloss over Juicebox's eyes. He clenched his fists and spit angry words back into the darkness. "We're coming for you!"

*"WE?"* The darkness scoffed at him.

"We'll destroy you!" Juicebox took a step forward, feeling the adrenaline of his desire to slaughter this beast.

A large, wide mouth filled with razor sharp teeth appeared beneath its glowing eyes. It laughed in Juicebox's face as he stumbled backwards, heart dipping into his chest with fear.

*"YOU CAN TRY YOUR BEST, BUT YOU WILL NOT SUCCEED. BESIDES, I DON'T THINK YOU REALLY WANT TO GET RID OF ME."*

"There isn't anything I want more." Juicebox spat back. Disgusted.

The darkness rose above him laughing. *"SOMEHOW THE STUPID BOY STILL CANNOT SEE. I WILL HELP HIM UNDERSTAND."* He chuckled to himself. *"I'VE SAID IT BEFORE BUT I SUPPOSE I MUST BE FORCED TO REPEAT MYSELF TIME AND TIME AGAIN TO YOU, JUICEBOX. YOU SEE, I AM EVERYWHERE!"*

The darkness made his full purple mass visible to Juicebox in the backdrop of black. It rose up like a terrifying ocean wave. *"I CAN BE AS BIG AS THE EARTH,"* The wave rose up impossibly high, hovering menacingly over Juicebox. *"OR AS SMALL AS A GRAIN OF SAND..."* The ocean of its mass crashed down on him. He hunched over, bracing himself from the impact as the darkness broke apart into a million tiny grains, scattering all around him, nearly burying him alive.

The sand started to swirl and gather with the twisting of a newly formed funnel cloud that extended as high as a skyscraper. Juicebox shielded his eyes from the sand flying around his face.

"I don't understand! How did you come out of me? How did I create such a monster?"

The tornado calmed again as Darkness gathered itself back to its monstrous form, floating quickly to meet Juicebox closely face to face.

*"YOU THINK THAT YOU CREATED ME?"* The monster laughed with genuine amazement. *"YOUR EGO HAS SUCH A STUNNING IMAGINATION! YOU REALLY THINK THAT YOU COULD HAVE CREATED SUCH A FORCE OF POWER LIKE ME?"* Its mouth clicked scoldingly at Juicebox.

"HAVEN'T I ALREADY TOLD YOU THAT YOU ARE NOTHING! WHEN IS THAT GOING TO FINALLY SINK INTO YOUR THICK, STUPID SKULL!" Juicebox furrowed his brow in confusion.

"YOU CREATE SOMETHING AS POWERFUL AS ME? HA. THAT JUST MIGHT BE THE MOST RIDICULOUS THING I HAVE EVER HEARD." The darkness turned from Juicebox. "NO. I HAVE BEEN WORKING ON THIS TOWN FOR A VERY, VERY LONG TIME. PATIENTLY FESTERING, SLOWLY CHOKING OUT THE LIFE OF EVERYONE AND EVERYTHING."

"You said I created this mess! You said that this was MY FAULT!" Juicebox yelled back at the beast.

The monster did not respond at first to Juicebox's outburst, keeping his back turned away. He sensed hesitation from the darkness as if it had been caught in a mistake or even a lie. It sunk back into the shadow again until Juicebox could only see the glow of its eyes staring out at him, and its evil grin widened just enough to show its rows of teeth.

Finally, it moved out of the shadow again and answered. "YES, WELL... YOU DID MAKE THIS MESS."

Juicebox narrowed his eyes at the beast. "I don't understand!"

*"OF COURSE, YOU DON'T. AND YOU NEVER WILL."* The monster sank back into the shadow.

"What are you?" Juicebox muttered under his breath.

The darkness was silent.

Juicebox glared unflinchingly at the darkness and screamed, "Tell me! What the hell are you!"

Suddenly the darkness was directly behind him, speaking softly into his ear. *"I'M THE FEELING YOU GET WHEN YOU TURN OUT THE LIGHT. THE WHISPERS YOU HEAR IN AN EMPTY ROOM."* The monster's voice shifted to his other ear.

*"I AM DESPAIR— DESPAIR OVER PEOPLE OR EVENTS, OR EVEN OVER NOTHING AT ALL."* He growled each word with disdain. *"WHEN I AM NOT DESPAIR, I AM PANIC. THAT UNPAID NOTICE IN THE MAIL, THE MISSED TELEPHONE CALL, THE NEWS YOU WERE HOPING WOULD NEVER COME...."* His voice heaved long and low.

*"I AM THE SINKING FEELING OF A CHEEK LEFT UNKISSED. I AM THERE WITH EVERY TEAR, EVERY BAD DAY, AND EVERY FAILED ATTEMPT!"* Juicebox could feel

the spit from the monster's speech and smell the foul breath of its mouth.

"*I AM THE SHADOW IN YOUR LIFE. THE SHADOW OVER ALL LIFE! AND EVEN ON THE DAYS YOU THINK EVERYTHING IS OKAY, I AM STILL THERE LOOKING OVER YOUR SHOULDER. WATCHING.*

*WAITING.*

*LOOMING.*

*HUNTING.*

*FOR YOU!*" The monster stretched open its mouth wide enough to swallow Juicebox whole. He screamed as he crouched down to be devoured by the beast.

¤¤¤

"Wake up! Hey, Juicebox! Wake up!" Stacy shouted at Juicebox as she violently shook his shoulders.

"Huh?" Juicebox's eyes rolled back into place and tried to focus on Stacy. His head pounded with explosive pressure. He pressed at the ache in his head with the palm of his hand, realizing he was back in the living room with his friends.

"Juicebox! Are you okay?" Stacy asked, clear concern in her voice. "You were out of it–like you were having some kind of seizure or something." He looked back and forth at his friends, letting their faces come fully into focus, then attacked them with a big bear hug.

"I knew you guys wouldn't leave me."

Jefferson patted his friend's back, confused. "Of course not..." Stacy squeezed tightly to Juicebox. "We've been here the whole time, Juice. What happened?"

Juicebox could feel tears welling in his eyes. He wiped at them and stood up, walking to the door. His friends followed behind him as the three made their way outside into the open air. Juicebox sat on the porch, breathing deeply to calm his shaking hands.

"There's something I have to tell you guys." He stared out into the madness of the town. "We're listening." Jefferson encouraged him on.

"I hear him." Juicebox rested his chin on his folded hands. "Not all the time, but often enough. I hear him talking to me." His gaze remained forward, refusing to meet the eyes of his friends.

Stacy's brows laced with confusion. "Him? You mean the monster from that very first night?"

Juicebox nodded. "Yes. The darkness. I hear his voice in my head. He tells me things about myself."

"What kinds of things?" Jefferson's voice sounded nervous.

"He tells me I'm weak. That this is all my fault and that I'll never be able to escape him. He shows me pictures in my mind. Horrible, terrible scenes. Sometimes they are things that aren't really real. But often they are. And it seems like every day more and more of them are coming true."

He looked down at the grass. A mutated spider bit into an unexpecting ladybug. He sighed and shifted his eyes away.

"Maybe we can use your connection to him to our advantage!" Jefferson encouraged. "Maybe we can get some sort of information from him. Discover his weaknesses!"

Juicebox thought back to the recent words from the darkness; "*You think that YOU created me? Your ego has such a stunning imagination! ...I have been working on this town for a very, very long time.*"

He didn't know exactly what the darkness meant. But this new insight flared a small new hope within Juicebox. "Maybe you're right." He replied to Jefferson. "Maybe we can use his conversations with me to our advantage." He stood up and stared at the pulsing mountain ahead of them with determination. "Grab a snack from your backpacks and let's eat on the road. We need to keep going.

Jefferson pulled out some bags of chips and tossed one to Juicebox and Stacy and the three friends started back down the path to the mountain. Stacy lagged a bit behind the boys, chewing slowly on her chips. A low voice rumbled in her ear.

"*YOU DIDN'T WANT TO SHARE YOUR SECRET WITH THE CLASS, STACY?*" She kicked a rock in the road, ignoring the voice. "*YOU WEAK, PATHETIC GIRL, LETTING*

*JUICEBOX GO ON THINKING THIS IS ALL HIS FAULT, WHEN YOU AND I BOTH KNOW THE TRUTH.*" Stacy's footing faltered and she stumbled in the road.

"*IT'S YOURS.*"

*"How frail the human heart must be—*
*A mirrored pool of thought. So deep*
*And tremulous an instrument*
*Of glass that it can either sing,*
*Or weep."*

-Sylvia Plath

"Eyes on the prize my friends. Eyes on the prize." Juicebox stared out ahead at the mountain. He didn't want to let it get out of his sight. He wanted to face this thing now, desperately needing this nightmare to come to an end.

A slimy, bumpy-skinned snake creature flew through the air above them and let out a loud screech.

The friends darted out of the way as it spewed venom from its mouth, clearly scouting the ground for prey. "Quick! Get off the road!" Jefferson yelled as the beast turned sharply in the air, making its way back for a second shot at nailing them with its poison. They all dove behind a nearby pile of debris and attempted to quiet their breathing to hide from the creature. It hovered nearby, dripping and flapping its giant bat-like wings.

It screeched again and began diving for their hiding spot.

"I give up!" A slurred voice yelled from somewhere down the road. The creature hissed and turned toward the sound of the voice. "I've tried and I've tried but nothing seems to work." A middle-aged man walked forward holding his arms up in a drunken surrender as he stumbled, falling to his knees. "I couldn't get ahead in the old world. And this new world?" He laughed stupidly. "There's not even a point in trying." He yelled the last word directly at the beast in the air.

He pushed himself back to his feet and took a big drink from the bottle in his hand. "So come and get me. I'm done fighting." With lightning speed, the creature darted toward the man and entered him through his nose. The massive size of the creature filled his body, bubbling and stretching it out. Slowly the man started to transform, taking the shape of a fleshy bottle covered in yellow-green skin. Liquid poured from his mouth like a never-ending keg.

Juicebox grabbed his friends' arms and urged them forward. "Quick! Run!" He yelled, seizing their chance to escape the horrific scene. The three friends jumped up and ran with all their might. They ignored any snarling, ugly moans on the road as they sprinted ahead, refusing to be distracted by any more monsters or mayhem, and ran and ran for what felt like hours, stopping only for water when their lungs felt like they were about to cave in.

"We've got…to keep…. going." Juicebox breathed encouragingly to his tired friends. They were covered in sweat, and losing momentum when they finally reached a crumbling building near the base of the mountain.

They snaked themselves behind the wall of the building and each fell to the ground in exhaustion.

"We are nearly there." Juicebox smiled as he splashed a water bottle in his face. They took a few minutes to just sit and breathe before rising to scope out their surroundings.

"There are more of those flying things," Stacy pointed out with concern. Twenty to thirty of the flying beasts circled the mountain protectively. "We'll have to think of some way to deal with those before we can make our way up or into the mountain." The three friends just sat for a while, thinking of what to do next.

Stacy stared off toward an old fence near the path. It was foggy and the area was covered with trees. *Pretty.* She thought. It reminded her of a misty hideaway. It looked like such a nice place to rest after their long run—so shady and refreshing. She continued to stare at it. A man approached the fence. He wore an old trucker hat, a faded denim work jumper, and had a friendly, sun-weathered face. "Dad?" she whispered as she rose to her feet.

Juicebox grabbed her hand. "Stacy, where are you going?" Stacy continued to stare at the man at the fence and tugged her hand free from Juicebox. "I just need to go look at something really quick." Juicebox and Jefferson were soon on their feet. "Wait, no Stacy. We are so close. We can't wander from the path now."

Jefferson nodded. "Let's figure out our plan first, Stace. Don't go wandering off now." Stacy ignored the pleas of her friends and started walking down the path to the fence. "Please just stay here and watch my back, okay? It will only be a second." She urged the boys. The earnestness of her expression quieted her friends. When Stacy wanted something, she got it. No questions asked. They sat back down and nodded at her. "Just be quick." Juicebox pleaded.

Stacy's eyes were single toward the man in the trucker hat. He seemed to notice her and then turned and walked away from the fence sending Stacy into a run. "Wait!" She cried out. "Dad?" She breached the shady fog and clasped her hands to the fence. "DAD!!!" She cried out into the mist.

Juicebox and Jefferson watched earnestly as Stacy jumped the fence and ran from their view. "Oh Stacy... " Juicebox sighed. "We gotta go after her." Jefferson wiped a tired hand down his face and moaned, nodding. The boys took off running toward their friend.

Stacy pranced through what now appeared to be a beautiful, shaded wood. "Dad!" She cried out repeatedly. "Please come back!" The wood felt like a portal to a completely different time and place. The sounds of crickets filled the air and fireflies danced above a lovely, still pond. The water was surrounded by trees that were coated with enchanted green moss. "I didn't know our city had this pond... What is this place..."

She stopped to peer at the water, unsure of which direction the man in the trucker hat went. An uneasy feeling gripped her as she realized she was completely alone in this unknown land. A large toad hopped past her, diving headfirst into the clear blue pond. "Ah!" Stacy jumped backward from the surprise of the toad. She clutched at her thumping heart, feeling a pang of guilt at the fright that her froggy prank must have given Mrs. Gill those few weeks ago. It felt like a lifetime since that day...

A twig snapped behind a nearby tree, and the man in the trucker hat stepped forward, out from the wood. "Hey Stace." Stacy's eyes locked with the eyes she loved most in this world. "Dad!" She rushed to him, jumping into his arms. She kissed his cheek and breathed in his smokey pine scent. She had missed that scent almost as much as she missed the feel of her father's arms around her after a long, hard day.

Tears streamed down her cheeks. "I've missed you so much. Why did you leave me?" She sobbed into the crook of his neck. Her father didn't answer her question, he just stood there holding her. She pulled away and looked back into his eyes. "Why are you here right now? I don't understand?" Her father smiled and wiped at her tears, patting her head back down to rest on his shoulder. He was silent. Stacy breathed in his scent again, but something was starting to smell off. She pulled away to look back into his eyes and stared deeply into them. Their usual shade of deep chocolate brown was speckled with a sickly, neon green.

She moved to back away from him. But her hands were stuck. "Dad? What's going on?" The smell of him grew more rancid, like fish left in a mailbox on a hot day. She coughed at the stench.

"What is this?! Let me go!" She couldn't get her hands unstuck from his arms. Before her eyes, the image of her dad was completely transformed and she saw that she was glued to a large, slimy tentacle by tiny suction cups. The tentacle had been camouflaged somehow, but she could now clearly see the base of it bulging out from the water of the pond. The once, still, clear blue water bubbled and boiled below, its color shifting from icy blue to muddy green.

A large head covered in flat, stringy hair began rising, bursting forth from the waters beneath. It was a bony looking woman with sharp shoulders and a large, pointed chin. She cackled like a fairytale witch, tearing her remaining tentacled legs up and out of the pond.

"*Oh child...*" The witch cooed as she lifted Stacy toward her face to get a good look at her. "*You know, I see it all the time but it still brings me such delight seeing how even the well-intended can stray from the path.*" She cackled again, her oil slicked strands of hair bouncing and dripping around her. Stacy kicked her boots at the tentacled leg that held her, feeling completely drenched with panic. "Let me go!" She kicked harder, driving the heel of her boot into the witch's rubbery flesh.

The witch leaned her pointy chin in toward Stacy with a mockingly pouty lip. *"Now, now... what would the fun in that be? I haven't even been able to show you the reason you were brought here. Come child and look into my pool..."* Stacy was suddenly plunged downward, overlooking the murky water with an inch of air to spare. The witch pointed a crooked finger toward the pool below.

*"Look and see..."*

Stacy peered into the water and immediately noticed green and pink lights glowing up at her. She stared harder and her eyes widened as she realized that they were not tiny lights, but pink eyed souls that were swimming up toward her near the surface. The souls spiraled and twisted in a sort of haunted dance. It was mesmerizing. She felt hypnotized by the sight of them and could not seem to break her eyes away.

"What are they?" Stacy asked in amazement. The witch leaned her face in closer to Stacy's. *"They are my collection. The souls of lost dreams."* Stacy shook her head, still unable to look away. "I don't understand…" The witch nodded knowingly, almost sympathetically and spoke calmly to Stacy in response.

"I am what some may call… a patron of the arts—the art of dreams. These souls come to me, and bare to me their woes. They show me the hopes in their hearts, their wishes on stars. They cry out to me with the pains of their unfulfilled plans." She tsked pitifully down at them. "I help them see more clearly."

Stacy stared into their faces as they became clearer. "They look sad." Stacy broke her gaze from the water and turned toward the witch. The witch's eyes pierced intensely through Stacy. *"They are not."* Stacy furrowed her brows at the witch. "How do you help them? What exactly is it that you do?" The woman smiled and Stacy saw her teeth covered in layers of old river moss.

*"I rid them of their burdens, strip them of their fears."*

It was then that Stacy noticed the large shining pearls that traced the outline of the witch's ears.

There were hundreds, even thousands of them glistening behind her stringy hair.

"You take away their dreams." The witch cocked an eyebrow at the girl. *"I give them what they want."*

"Which is?" Stacy glared at her.

*"Lack of feeling."*

The witch bent a knobby finger down into the pool and tapped it. It let off a sound like a gong going off underwater and Stacy was suddenly plunged into the murky depths as images began playing out in front of her. It was a memory. "Is that me?!" *Little Stacy sat happily on her dad's tool bench, swinging her legs and chatting away to her dad who was working underneath an old car.*

*"Hey Stace, could you hand me that other crescent wrench I had set to the side?" Little Stacy flashed a gap-toothed smile and walked the tool over to the old Geo Metro, placing it into her dad's strong, roughened hand. He slid out from underneath the car and wiped his face with a towel. "You know, Ms. Stacy, I think we may just get this old thing going again by the end of the day!" His voice was so*

cheerful. It made Stacy feel so safe, and happy—warm from head to toe.

"What a beautiful memory." The witch cooed as Stacy stared, entranced by the images in front of her. "My dad was a mechanic." Stacy replied as if under a spell. "He always worked for other people but it was his dream to open up his own shop someday. My dream too, in fact. We always talked about doing it together when I got older." Stacy's eyes slowly moved out of focus as a glowing pink light began to spiral into her irises. The witch nodded sympathetically.

*"Tell me what else you see."*

Stacy's small smile faded.

"I see the day my dad left."

*Her mom had been screaming all morning, going through one of her many, "episodes." She didn't know what caused them. Dad always said they weren't her fault though, and that they just needed to be patient with her. Stacy had been tuning out the noise as usual, hiding behind her bedroom door with her palms pressed firmly to her ears. She waited patiently for her father to come into her room and tell her that everything was okay, like he always did after mom's bad days. Maybe today he would take her out of the house and they'd go get some ice cream, or maybe they would spend the rest of the day together at the shop. Her dad always knew what to do to make sure she felt safe. He was her light in the darkness, her fire of warmth during the blizzards of her life.*

*Stacy waited.*

*And waited.*

*Dad was taking longer than usual to come to her rescue.*

*She heard mom's screaming make its way outside as a car door shut loudly in the driveway. She rushed to her window to see what was happening. Dad was sitting in the front seat of his truck. He turned his key, lighting the ignition and Stacy bolted from her room and out the front door.*

*"Dad!!!" She screamed. Mom was rushing in and out of the house now, throwing dad's clothes, still on hangers, towards his truck in a fury. Dad's truck screeched from the driveway. "DAD!!!!" Stacy screamed. He never looked back at her, never turned the truck around. Mom stomped on dad's clothes in*

the driveway, mascara streaming down her face as her bitter words slurred incoherently from her lips. Stacy suddenly felt exposed, completely on display to the world. Neighbors were peeking their eyes through windows and poking their heads out of doors to examine the scene. Stacy bolted back inside and slammed the door to her room, falling to her knees with her back pressed firmly to the door as she heaved a heavy, uncontrollable sob.

Dad had never left her alone during mom's episodes. She was hurt and scared and felt the biting pangs of unexpected betrayal. She forced herself to calm her breathing and think rationally. He would be back. Surely within the next hour or two he'd be back. He would apologize. He would have a reason for doing what he did. She tore out her headphones from her nightstand and flopped herself onto her bed to drown out the chaos as she waited.

And waited.

And waited.

Night came and she waited.

Weeks passed and she waited.

*But as Summer faded into Autumn, and Autumn into Winter, leaves fell and died withering on the ground along with all hope and trust she had ever possessed within her heart.*

*She racked her brain for reasons why he could have left her, but nothing ever seemed to make total sense. If he was sick of mom's rampages, of course he would want to leave, but why didn't he take her with him? Why would he leave her alone to deal with such chaos? Why wouldn't he say something to her first? Leave a note? Write her a letter to explain?*

*She landed on what felt like the only plausible explanation—he didn't love her enough to care. Of course. This rationale brought all the puzzle pieces together into a painfully perfect picture. For whatever reason, dad decided he didn't care about her anymore. He was able to turn a blind eye to her pain and never look back.*

*And she hated him for it.*

*Locking away the key to her heart, Stacy built up walls for protection, high as the hills. She decked herself with spikes and chains, pierced herself with daggers and blades, and painted her eyes as dark as* she felt, daring anyone who crossed her path to just try and hurt her. She had already been through hell, and there was no soul alive who could give her any pain worse than what she had already experienced, not that she would even let them get close enough to try.

Her mom got the closest by drinking more than ever as soon as dad left them, and bringing deadbeat boyfriend after deadbeat boyfriend into the house no matter how many times Stacy begged her to stop. But Stacy was determined to never let this affect her. She didn't care enough. She wouldn't care enough.

Reliving these memories was torture. "Stop." Stacy demanded. "Make it stop!"

The witch raised Stacy out from the memory pool and stared deeply into her eyes. Stacy was shivering with cold and pain, and heartache. The images she just witnessed had torn down all the walls she worked so hard to build and had pierced through her very heart. She cried out with pain. "JUST PLEASE, MAKE IT STOP." She begged, sobbing. The witch tsked at her pitifully. *"I know it hurts…"*

She shushed at Stacy's cries with tenderness. "I can help."

She lowered her to the water again.

"Just give me your old dreams. They are already lost to time and circumstance, never to be fulfilled. Hand them to me and I will keep them nice and safe for you. In return, I will remove all pain. You will never have to feel this way again." She pointed to the souls in the water. "You can be free. Free to float and bask in my waters, rid of every heartache forever."

It sounded like heaven—a dream come true.

The witch leaned closer to whisper in her ear. "You will no longer have to try so hard to guard your heart, child. I will guard it for you."

Stacy nodded, feeling peaceful already. She was ready to let go of her dreams. It's not like her dad was ever going to come back anyways. She was ready to float away. The water called to her and she reached for it, the witch held her back.

"Remember, you must first give me your dreams. Then you will be free. You must allow me to reach inside of you to grab them. Do you agree?"

Stacy opened her mouth to speak when she heard screaming from the edge of the pond. It was Juicebox and Jefferson. "Stacy, no! Stop!" They yelled at her. Juicebox was picking up rocks and chucking them at the witch. They bounced off her giant body with ease. The witch hissed and then collected herself. *"Hush boys!" She called out. "I am helping your friend! I can help you too if you give me but a moment..."*

Juicebox jumped into the water and swam for the witch. "Stacy! Fight back!" He cried out. "What are you doing?!" Stacy turned tiredly to face her swimming friend. "She's right, Juicebox! She is going to help me. She is going to take away my pain. I can't go on with it, Juice. She's going to make it all better."

Juicebox swam faster, kicking at the souls below him that started to grab at his ankles. "Stacy, just wait!" He had almost reached one of the witch's large tentacles. She scooped him up roughly. *"Look boy, I can help you too. But first we must assist your friend Stacy here."*

Stacy pointed down into the water. "Look, Juicebox. See those floating souls? They are completely free from pain. Poof! Gone." Juicebox looked down into the water and gasped. "Stacy, those things look haunted!" The witch laughed. *"It's just the opposite. I remove all that haunts them."*

"All you have to do, Juice, is give her your lost dreams. And she will take away all the pain. Wouldn't it be amazing to never have to feel the hurt from your parents' death? Wouldn't it be so great to have all of this mess just disappear? She can do that for us!" Stacy was smiling at him hopefully.

Juicebox stared back down at the souls.

"Stacy, something isn't right. They might not be feeling any pain but it definitely doesn't look like they are feeling any joy either!" The witch's mouth twitched at his words. Stacy stared thoughtfully at the souls. "If there's one thing we've learned throughout this entire journey, it's that things are constantly trying to trap us, Stacy! We need to leave! You need to fight!"

Stacy stared at the witch. The glimmering pearls that dangled from her saggy ears were so beautiful. As she peered at them, they filled her with a desire to dream and wish and hope. "Can I touch one of those?" Stacy reached out to grab at one of the pearls. The witch's eyes instantly blared with fury and she tossed her to the edge of the pond, still clutching tightly to Juicebox. Stacy landed on the muddy ground with a splat and Jefferson ran to her side.

The witch made quick business of mussing her stringy hair in front of her ears to try to hide the shining pearls. *"Nobody touches these. You may not even LOOK at them."* Stacy narrowed her eyes at the witch, the pull she had to the water was gone as if an enchantment had been lifted. "Those are the dreams aren't they? Those are the lost hopes and wishes of the souls in the water."

The witch cackled. *"What they are... is mine."* Stacy threw a rock, hitting the witch square in her crooked nose. "You tricked those people! You show them the worst parts of their life so that they will trade the most precious parts of themselves to just stop feeling anything! You lie!" The witch lunged herself forward to the edge of the pond, to stare straight into Stacy's eyes. *"I tell them exactly what I will do. Just like I told you. They give me their dreams of their own free will."*

Stacy could feel tears stinging in her eyes. "Do they even remember? Do they have any recollection of what they lost once you take it from them? If I would have given you my lost dreams, would I still remember my dad's face?" The witch turned away. *"You would receive what I told you. Freedom from pain."*

Stacy knew what she needed to do. She turned off her anger, and resumed her previously dazed, and complacent manner. "Put my friend down. He will never give you what you want." The witch cocked a brow at her. "But I will." She held her arms up for the witch to take hold of her again.

"NOOOOO!" Juicebox and Jefferson both cried in unison. The witch popped Juicebox onto the ground and swooped Stacy back into the air. *"I knew that you were such a wise child."* The witch purred. *"So far beyond your years."* She brought Stacy close to her face and peered deeply into her eyes. *"This will only hurt for a moment."* She raised a crooked finger above her chest and closed her eyes, concentrating deeply. As she did so, Stacy slowly reached behind herself for her bat, its handle sticking out of her backpack for easy access. She clutched at it and lunged forward with all of her might, swinging hard at the witch's ear.

The witch shrieked as glimmering pearls cascaded freely down into the water below. Stacy made another swipe at the ear but was shoved deep into the waters of the pool. Souls circled around her like ghosts. She began to swim upwards to the surface but the souls clutched at her and began dragging her down further into the depths. She screamed out her breath, the last of her air flowing out of her mouth in bubbles around her.

The witch was thrashing in the water above. Stacy's vision blurred as the souls released their grip on her, rushing to examine the pearls that sunk around them like beautiful glowing stars. Consciousness escaped her as she floated in this haunted sea.

Juicebox dove into the water once more, pushing past souls that were eagerly clambering for pearls. He caught sight of Stacy sinking downward, her eyes glowing a wild shade of pink. He grabbed her hand and pulled her upward as he struggled for breath, dodging at the witch's thrashing tentacles above. Reaching the surface, he gasped for air and dragged Stacy onto the muddy bank of the pond.

He immediately began to thrust his hands on Stacy's chest to give her CPR. Her eyes were still open, glowing with that fiery pink. "Come on Stacy, wake up!" Jefferson hovered above them calling her name. Water and moss spurted from her mouth as she coughed and blinked away the glow from her eyes.

Juicebox and Jefferson sighed in relief and swarmed her with tenderness. "Are you alright, Stace?" Juicebox saw now that her head was bleeding. He ripped part of his hoodie and held it to her wound. "I'm good…" She was dazed as she stared out into the pond. The witch was still thrashing and screaming as she searched the waters for her pearls. In a moment, people started exiting from the depths, climbing up the witch's tentacles in droves. *"Back!!! Back you fiends!!!"* She screamed at them, swatting them away.

"The people reclaimed their lost dreams when they fell into the water!" Juicebox cried, surprised. "It looks like they are trying to free the rest of them now!" The men and women who emerged from the depths climbed the witch's body. She swatted at them like ants but she was outnumbered by a longshot. They clawed at her ears and pearls fell like jewels from the sky. The more that fell, the weaker and smaller she became, sinking lower and lower into the pond.

"It looks like they've got the witch covered." Jefferson said under his breath. Stacy nodded and coughed up more water. "I think you're right. Our work here is done. We need to get back on the path." The friends stood to leave, walking quickly from the terrible scene. Stacy looked back as the pond faded slowly from view. The bony hand of the witch grasped upward out of the water, and slowly sunk down beneath the surface.

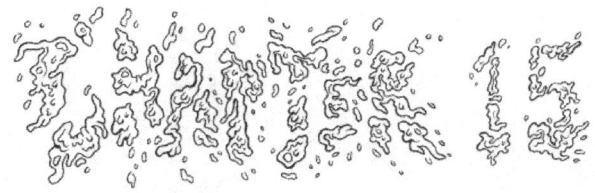

# CHAPTER 15

*"Today is your day, your mountain is waiting. So, get on your way."*

*- Dr. Seuss*

The friends stopped at the edge of the wood. The mountain could be seen vaguely through the mist still surrounding them. The sun was setting low into the sky. "I don't think we'll be able to scale that thing before dark." Juicebox said, leaning against the fence. "Definitely not. And we still need a plan on how to handle those flying beasts." Jefferson agreed. Stacy dug through her wet backpack for some food. "We need to decide where we should set up camp for the night. It's either that crumbling building straight ahead, or underneath one of these trees here."

The decision was an easy one. The mist still felt so refreshing from the blaring pink sun of the day, and provided the friends with some level of protection from anything that might be lurking down the road. They huddled together underneath a large oak tree and snacked on their remaining packages of food. Juicebox kept his eyes on the pulsing mountain peeking through fog as he ate, as if looking away would just lead him off on some new side quest once again. He felt focused and determined to scale the thing as soon as he reached it.

"I think that I need to climb it alone." He said as he chomped on his oatmeal cream cookie. Stacy and Jefferson looked at him as if he were a madman. "That's really funny Juicebox." Stacy replied flatly. Jefferson rolled his eyes. "Yeah man, how could that possibly be a good idea?" Juicebox kept his eyes ahead. "I think it might be the only way to do it. In order for someone to make it up that mountain, those flying things need to be taken care of. And the only way I can see that happening is if you guys are down below distracting them."

It made sense. But they didn't like it. "At least let us try to do both. We can go up a bit slower behind you and distract them as we try to slowly scale it. Meanwhile you can get a head start and try to climb as fast as you can. Eventually, we might catch up to you." Stacy looked at Jefferson for support. "I'm Team Stacy." He said through a mouthful of pretzels.

Juicebox pondered the idea. "I still think you guys would be safer if you stayed on the ground. It would give you more places to hide from those things." He finally glanced at his friends. Their faces were determined and he could see that their minds were already made up. He nodded at them. "I guess we'll just give it a shot and see."

¤¤¤

The friends were silent as they ate and rested from yet another long, tumultuous day. Juicebox rubbed at his head thinking through his plans for tomorrow. Anxiety flooded through him as he pondered what he would do when he reached the top of the mountain. What horrors would he find? How was he going to battle the darkness that inhabited it?

Juicebox closed his eyes and ran down the corridors of his mind for answers, eventually stumbling upon the image of his parents. His initial reaction was to push it away. The visualization of his parents' faces still brought so much pain. So much guilt. So much longing. He took another deep breath and brought the image back to the forefront of his mind. *"What do I do?"* He silently pleaded as he allowed himself to think back on the life he once lived, back when everything was normal and natural and comfortable.

A memory flooded in of his dad sitting at his side at the kitchen table, helping him with his math homework.

*Despite Dad already using three alternate ways to show Juicebox how to figure out the problem, it still just wasn't clicking in his mind. He felt like he wanted to scream. "I just don't get it, dad. None of this makes any sense."*

Juicebox buried his head into his arms on the table, crumpling the worksheet that lay beneath him. Dad placed a warm, reassuring hand on his sulking back. "Don't worry, son." He squeezed his shoulder. "We just need to find the explanation of the problem that works for you." Juicebox shook his head in his arms as he attempted to choke back the emotion he felt growing in his chest. "But why? Why can everyone else just sit in class and understand the first time that the teacher explains how to do the equation, and I have to sit at the table every night with my dad as we go through a million different ways to make my stupid brain understand."

Dad took a deep breath. "You're not stupid, Juicebox." Juicebox shot his head up and met his dad's eyes. "Then what am I?" His face was red and blotchy with frustration and his voice shook as he thought of how easily everyone else in his class was able to get through their school day. Dad took off his glasses and pinched the bridge of his nose. Juicebox rolled his eyes thinking that Dad was growing tired of his complaining as usual. But Dad suddenly smiled and chuckled deeply, eyes still closed in thought.

"You're brilliant, actually." He leaned forward towards Juicebox's confused face and smiled at him. "You're absolutely brilliant."

"What are you talking about?" Juicebox stared wide eyed at his dad, stunned out of his frustration. "Juicebox!" Dad laughed again. "If you could only see yourself the way that your mother and I see you. The things you can do are things that I would have never been able to dream of. Your stories. Your drawing. Even your skateboarding! I could never do what you do."

Juicebox shrugged. "Anybody can learn how to do those things." Dad chuckled again. "Just like anybody can learn how to do this math problem." He pointed to the crumpled worksheet. Juicebox shook his head. "It's not the same... " Dad interrupted. "It's exactly the same." He put his hand on Juicebox's shoulder again. "We all have things that come naturally to us, son. It's okay that math isn't that natural skill for you." Dad grabbed a piece of paper from Juicebox's notebook and drew a stick figure. "This... " He pointed at the drawing. "Is the extent of my drawing skills." Juicebox looked down at the sad little man on the paper and let out a laugh.

"Rude..." Dad winked at him. "Come on dad..." Juicebox chuckled. Dad laughed along with him. "I'm being serious! This is as good as I can do. Now what would you do to help me turn this drawing into a warrior you'd feel proud to tape to your bedroom wall?" Juicebox took a deep breath in. "Well... you could start by giving him some shoulders... some muscles... try giving the body some volume by using more than one line to make up each of his limbs... " Dad followed his instructions on the paper and held up his new creation. "Like this?" The image on the paper was somehow worse and more ridiculous than the one before. Juicebox couldn't help but laugh again.

"Now what?" Dad smiled at him. Juicebox covered his face with his hand. "I think we'd just have to go back and start with the basics." Dad put the paper onto the table and bit at the pencil in his hand. "I was afraid you'd say that." He tapped his leg as if deep in thought. "Which do you reckon would take longer... you understanding this math problem, or me figuring out how to turn this odd mess into a beautiful work of art?"

Juicebox stared down at the problem in front of him, then shifted his eyes to Dad's drawing and chuckled again. "You're going to say the math problem aren't you?" Dad cocked his brow at him. Juicebox smirked and nodded. "Probably." Dad nodded in understanding. "That's what I thought." He laid the pencil back down on Juicebox's worksheet and stared into his eyes. "Not everything comes naturally in life, Juicebox. Sometimes we run into tough problems to solve. They may take some time, or reflection from different perspectives. They might require that we go back to the basics. But they can be solved. Be patient with yourself."

Juicebox took a deep breath and lifted his pencil once more. "Okay." He breathed. "Let's try again."

The memory swirled and shifted into another.

Juicebox watched as his mother placed an oversized mason jar onto the kitchen counter. She had a sparkle in her eye and the overwhelming air of hopefulness lingered around her. "What's the jar for?" Juicebox asked as he chomped on a slice of delicious banana bread he had swiped from the kitchen just moments before. Mom hummed happily and cracked some eggs into the large bowl of batter she had been working on. "Mom?" Juicebox questioned again, trying to break his mother's trance. "Oh... what was that, sweetheart?" She smiled at him as she dumped chocolate chips into the bowl.

"What's the jar for?" He questioned again, motioning to the glass. Mom's smile grew wider. "That... " She began, "Is our new vacation fund." She finished stirring the batter and began spooning careful ladles of the mixture into bread pans. "Which I will be funding... " She bent over to stick the pans into the oven, "With my new business."

Juicebox raised his eyebrows. "Ahhh... new business, eh?" He walked over to the counter and sliced himself another piece of the cakey deliciousness. "You're finally going to be sharing your baking wizardry with the world I'm guessing?" Mom smiled at him. "Yes. But just banana bread for now! Until I can expand... " Juicebox chuckled. "Wow! Sounds like you've got some big plans! I need to design you some business cards!" Mom's eyes lit up at his words. "Oh, would you, Juice? That would just be perfect!"

Juicebox stuffed the last of his slice into his mouth. "Of course! But I'll need payment." Mom raised a suspicious eyebrow at him. He laughed. "I will require at least a few slices of your product per day. In perpetuity." Mom's smile brightened the room. "Done."

She began to wash the dishes she had been working with. As Juicebox watched her scrub he noticed that her knuckles were dried and cracked. He walked over to the sink and gently shooed her away to rest as he took the dishes from her hands. She fought him for a split second before conceding and resting herself against their small kitchen butcher block.

"So where are we going?" Juicebox asked as he loaded several bowls and whisks into the dishwasher. "Hmm? Oh! On vacation?" His mother asked dreamily, still lost in her thoughts. "Yes, on vacation." Juicebox chuckled. Mom sighed and tapped her chin as she pondered his question.

"Disneyland... Hawaii... Chatsworth House... " Juicebox squinted his eyes at her. "Chatsworth House?" Mom stopped her daydreamy staring and met his eyes. "Oh, you know! It's the filming location of Mr. Darcy's Pemberly!" Juicebox tilted his head at her. "I'm not following." Mom swatted a towel at him from behind. "From Pride and Prejudice!"

Juicebox laughed. "Right, right, right. How could I forget about Mr. Darcy's Pemberly? Sounds like the perfect family vacation." Mom smiled and moved toward Juicebox, putting her hand on his shoulder in earnest. "Oh, but it would be! We could even start a separate fund to begin saving to hire a historical costume designer! We could all go to Pemberly dressed like we were from 1813!"

Juicebox dropped the dishes he was scrubbing and turned to face her with his mouth agape. Mom's giggle filled the deliciously scented kitchen and Juicebox couldn't help but laugh with her. He nodded. "I always have thought I'd look rather dashing in a cravat... " Mom kissed his cheek. "You would!"

*As the weeks passed, the contents of Mom's savings jar began to grow, and bananas began covering every inch of their kitchen countertops. Mom was a hustler. She printed off hundreds of the business cards Juicebox designed for her and left them with every person she came into contact with each day. Grocery clerks, delivery drivers, speed walkers she passed by on her morning workouts... every one of them was blessed with a business card from the smiley banana bread lady with a pep in her step and a twinkle in her eye.*

*But as the weeks turned into months, the contents of the jar began to fade. One month it was spent on a leak that they found underneath the bathroom sink that had started to mold. Another month the money was handed to the tire repair shop and come December Juicebox could only guess it was spent on the new game console he opened that chilly Christmas morning.*

*Despite her setbacks mom kept baking, and the jar somehow started to return to its previous state of growth. Juicebox noticed it one morning out of the corner of his eye before he went to school and smiled* as he noticed that it was nearly full. A sense of pride in his mom filled his chest as he set out for school that morning. But by the time he returned home something had changed. The jar on the counter was completely empty, and a gnawing sadness took over the usual scent of chocolate and bananas. Mom was crumpled on the couch, her face in her hands, quietly crying.

"Mom? What's wrong? What happened?" Juicebox walked over to her, wrapping an arm around her shoulders as he sank into the couch beside her. "I'm fine." she replied, blowing her nose into a tissue. "Obviously not, mom. What happened?" Mom just shook her head, not answering him. It was then that he noticed that it was incredibly hot inside their house. He walked over to the thermostat to click on the air. "Mom, it says it's ninety degrees in here... " He tapped at the little arrows on the box to try to turn the temperature down. The screen just blinked at him in mockery.

"It's broken, Juice. Don't try messing with it. I have somebody coming to work on it later this evening." She blew her nose again and wiped at the mascara running down her cheeks. "Oh mom… " Juicebox went back to her side. "I'm so sorry. The jar was nearly full… " Mom leaned her head on his shoulder and took in a shaky breath. "I want to say it's okay but… " Her voice cracked as she tried to continue, "I was just so close. I was right there… " She sobbed again.

Juicebox rubbed her back and patted her hand. "It's okay mom… you can do this. It will take some time but you've done it once, right? You can totally do this again… " Mom shook her head in his shoulder. "There's just always something… I need to take a break for a while." She got up and started opening windows to let in the breeze.

That week there were no bananas on the countertops, and no giggles of Mr. Darcy or Disneyland in the kitchen. There was no pep in Mom's step, and definitely no twinkle in her eye. But there were cinnamon pancakes on the table every morning. And a tender kiss on Juicebox's cheek every night before bed. There was her warm and calming presence after school as she let Juicebox vent about his day, and her words of love and reassurance at every turn. He could tell that Mom was sad. But she kept going. How did she keep going? She was crushed and he knew it. And yet... she was still doing life. How? The question began to gnaw at him.

He returned from school one day and found her at the table, silently writing in her journal. "Hi, honey. How was everything today?" She asked as he walked through the front door and set down his skateboard. Normally Juicebox would start his daily vent session about his assignments and teachers but he pushed it away today. "It was... fine." He pulled up a chair across from her and sat down. "Mmm... that's good, sweetheart." She kept her eyes on her journal and kept writing.

"Can I ask you something, mom?" She looked up from her journal and nodded. "Of course. What is it, Juicebox?" Juicebox hesitated for a moment trying to find the right words, afraid of sounding rude. "Well... you've just been super down since the AC went out and... " Mom interrupted him. "I know, honey, I'm sorry I-" Juicebox shook his head. "No, mom you don't need to apologize. I'm not mad at you. I'm impressed by you. I don't understand how you can keep going on and taking care of everything when you're feeling so down. I mean you worked so hard for so long and... I guess what I'm trying to ask is how do you do it? How do you keep going when you feel so sad?"

Mom looked stunned by the question and leaned over the table to take his hand. "Sometimes bad things happen, Juicebox. And you might not ever know why. And it might not ever be fair. But you have to keep going." She rubbed his hand with her thumb. Juicebox wrinkled his brow. "Yeah but I still don't understand. When I get super down I feel like I'm completely lost. How do you know what to do?" He asked. She smiled at him. "Sometimes you don't." A tear fell down her cheek. "So, you just start by just trying to do the things you do know. Get up in the morning. Brush your teeth. Take a shower. Make breakfast. Take care of your daily responsibilities. Let time pass as you do what you need to and see if that feels right. Then give it a good think and add in other things that feel right. And you just keep going, trusting that your heart will tell you what you need and what to do next."

He didn't remember when exactly it was after that. But eventually mom's eyes started to dream again. And bananas began piling on the kitchen counter once more.

Juicebox laid his head down on his backpack in the dirt and pondered on these memories. His parents' love and words running through his mind sent a calm through his body. *I'll try to be patient with myself.* He silently thought. *And I'll just start by doing what I know. I'll climb. And trust that I'll know how to face anything that comes after that.*

Sleep was sneaking up on him. It was getting cold as the sun faded away. He squished himself closer to Stacy and Jefferson for warmth. They placed their arms over each other in the dark and drifted off to sleep together.

¤¤¤

Juicebox awoke to the sound of a backpack zipping sharply. Stacy stood in the glow of the fluorescent sky and tossed him a candy bar. "Saved you the last one." She smiled at him. Jefferson was snoring next to him, drool pooling on his sweatshirt. Juicebox broke the bar into three and stuffed one of the pieces into Jefferson's open mouth, waking him with a jolt. "Hey!" He yelled and then tasted the chocolate on his mouth and sighed, swallowing his share in a single gulp.

Juicebox tossed the third piece to Stacy and shook the dirt from his pants as he rose to stand. "Today's the day," he breathed. Jefferson stood as well and wrapped an arm around his shoulder. "Whatever we face out there today, we can take it on together. We're gonna make it." Stacy nodded and nudged her head toward the fence. "I hear some crazy noises out there. Let's go get 'em."

Energized, the friends hopped the fence and exited the misty hideaway. At the sight of the mountain Juicebox felt another painful pang in his stomach. He hunched over and clutched at the pain that radiated from his middle. "Ah!" He cried out, holding up a hand to keep his friends from rushing to him. He stood again. "I'm fine." He said before they questioned him. "I'm getting—AH!" He hunched at the pain again. "... used to them..." He mumbled. Stacy and Jefferson just nodded as they continued their walk.

Surrounding the base of the mountain they saw strange creatures moving slowly around. They approached the area behind the crumbling building wall and scoped them out. They were definitely monsters, most likely townspeople that had been morphed by the darkness. But these monsters were slow, like tired zombies that only half-heartedly seemed to be on the prowl. "I think we can just run past those guys." Jefferson said. The friends agreed then looked up.

"It's still those guys up there that look like they'll be our greatest threat." Stacy pointed at the flying snake-like beasts. Juicebox surveyed the area again. It looked like there was a giant dead flying beast lying near the base of the mountain. "I think I have an idea. Follow me." Juicebox led the gang quickly to the mountain's base. They quietly swerved by the long, extended arms of the warped townspeople as they ran. They were right. Those guys were no trouble. Juicebox crouched down by the carcass to make sure the monster was really dead.

There was no doubt.

He tilted it upward to look underneath. The beast's guts had been dug out by some other creature and scraped clean. Its ribs showed through a web of dried flesh that had been picked at by something that must have been hungry nearby. "Hurry and climb in." He told his friends. They stared at him blankly. Jefferson whispered out a laugh. "No no no.. you're kidding me right?" Juicebox rolled his eyes and stepped beneath the monster's shell of a body. Stacy made a face and followed him inside. They could see Jefferson's feet hopping nervously beneath the leathery wings of the beast. He let out a grunt and joined the duo inside. "Out of all the things I thought we might face today; I didn't have wearing a smelly dead monster on my list!" He complained.

Juicebox lifted his t-shirt to cover his nose. "If you've got a better idea I'd be happy to hear it." Jefferson just whined and made a sound like he was gagging. "Can I at least not be in the butt?" Stacy kicked him in the shin. "Shut up Jefferson! The last one in the corpse gets the smelly butt. Now let's go!"

They lifted the carcass on their shoulders and began their climb upward onto the pulsing purple flesh, kicking at mutated rats and bugs as they climbed. "This is working pretty good!" Stacy laughed. She looked back at Jefferson who had stuffed two tampons up his nose to block out the smell. Her knees buckled at the sight, almost causing the friends to fall backwards down the mountain and lose the progress they had made. "Where in the world did you get those?!" She half yelled; half whispered trying to hold in her laughter. "The front pocket of your backpack." Jefferson's voice was nasally from the blockage. Juicebox looked back at his friend and groaned.

"Focus guys. This hurts." He stopped his walking and clenched at his stomach in pain with one hand, nearly dropping the carcass onto his head. Stacy and Jefferson caught his end of the beast and shifted their weight to keep it from crashing onto their friend. "I'm so sorry, Juicebox. I know. Let's keep going. We're getting there." Stacy nudged him forward and shot a glare back at Jefferson, the sight of him bringing a silent chuckle to her chest. She committed in that moment to not look back at him again. His nonsense was proving to be too risky a sight on this climb.

The friends walked onward and upward for what felt like miles, the hike getting steeper and steeper as they went. The corpse, while an excellent disguise, was proving to become quite a nuisance as they trekked forward. It was just getting way too heavy to continue to carry up the slope. They were drenched in sweat and fatigue as a disgusting beast ran toward them, snorting and squealing like a wild, mutated hog. Juicebox kicked at it and the monster bit into his foot. "AGH!" He yelled. Stacy crouched down and dove out of the carcass with her bat, smashing the beast swiftly in the head before clambering back inside the disguise with her friends.

They moved forward, Juicebox now limping slightly from the bite, and all three friends slumped lower and lower from the weight of the beast they carried.

"I don't think we can climb past this ledge with this thing." Juicebox said through gritted teeth. The team agreed and they moved to the ground to sit for a moment to think. Juicebox peeked his head out from under the beast and looked up. "Look!" he exclaimed quietly. "I see an opening up there, close to the top." He pointed to a small cave-like opening toward the tip of the mountain. "That's got to be how we can get in…"

Stacy and Jefferson peered out at the hole. "There's creatures crawling out of it!" Stacy whispered. "Crawling is an interesting description… it's more like they're pouring out of it." Jefferson mumbled in shock. Oozy monsters filed out of the cave in droves. Some made their way down the mountain and began entering the town, while others stayed around, crowding the opening. Juicebox's heart sank at the sight. "How are we going to do this? There are hundreds of them…" He wiped at the sweat that streaked down his face.

"We're gonna have to find some way to get this carcass up there. It's our only disguise. I don't see any way around it." The friends nodded. "I think that we might need to carry it from the outside for a while so we can get it over this ledge."

"Do you think that we can do it fast enough though?" Stacy asked. "Those flying things are even closer now," the beasts above shrieked wildly in the sky. "We can't let them see us."

"I don't think we have any other options." Juicebox said with a breath. Slowly and quietly, the friends lifted the beast and set it down on the pulsating flesh of the mountain. They each grabbed a side and moved to heft it over the ledge. It was heavy, its wings were floppy and awkward, and the ledge was angled oddly making it no easy task. They nearly dropped it down the side of the cliff twice before finally securing it in place.

"Okay," Juicebox whispered. Now let's get over this thing quickly! He and Jefferson laced their hands together to create a step for Stacy and raised her up over the ledge, then Juicebox went down on his hands and knees to give Jefferson a boost. With Stacy and Jefferson now safe on the edge, they reached down to help pull Juicebox upwards.

A loud screech sounded from above. "No!" Stacy cried out at the sight. One of the flying monsters was flapping near them. They needed to get

Juicebox up quickly. "You always had the clammiest damn hands... " Jefferson grunted as he tried to keep hold of Juicebox's grip. The flying beast screeched louder. "PULL!" Stacy whispered frantically. Juicebox was slipping. He looked below himself and caught sight of a small foothold. He secured his foot and lurched himself upward so his friends could grab tightly to his elbows. The tactic was successful. They pulled Juicebox up and all three scrambled back into the dead beast, continuing forward to the opening of the cave.

The walk was becoming increasingly steep and the friends had to take synchronized steps in order to keep tiny rocks from sending them back down the mountain. The muscles in their legs burned, and the pain in Juicebox's gut grew stronger and stronger. Monsters passed them on the path but the disguise seemed to be working. Nothing paid them any attention as they continued on their climb.

Eventually, the body of the beast whacked into something hard and firm. Juicebox peeked his head out to see what they hit. They had arrived at what appeared to be a giant wall of trash and debris. He looked around to find another way up but there was nothing. They were at a complete standstill.

Juicebox shook his head with frustration. "We've hit a wall. There is no other way up. We need to scale it." He sat for a moment to dig through his backpack. "I understand if you guys want to stay here. We aren't going to have any disguise moving forward and the wall is super steep. It's going to be tough and monsters are definitely going to see us on our way." Stacy and Jefferson peered out to take a look then stared at Juicebox with concern.

"We're coming. Let's go."

The team ditched the carcass and began to scale the wall of trash. It was pretty firmly packed for the most part, but occasionally pieces of debris would fall loose and topple down the side.

"Agh!" Stacy yelled as the sharp lid of a tin can cut at her leg. "Are you okay?!" Jefferson and Juicebox looked down at her as she moaned in pain. Blood dripped down her leg, falling in big droplets onto the ledge below. Stacy breathed through the pain. "Keep climbing." She urged them forward, the frustration from her pain biting through into her tone.

Mutated maggots and worms poked their nasty heads out through their handholds trying to attack, causing the kids to endure a never-ending game of whack-a-mole amidst their difficult climb.

It was steep.

It was hard.

The kids were shaking from the incredible strain on their teenage arms and legs. Each pull upward felt like a shot of Jello into their limbs, weakening and jiggling at their efforts. By the time they finally reached the top, they could hardly fill their lungs with a single breath.

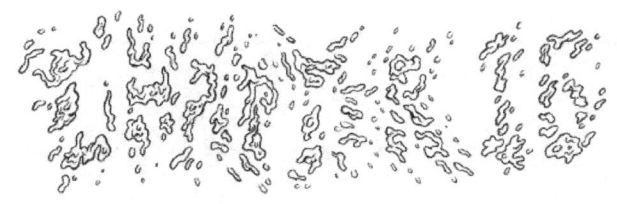

*"You could stand me up at the gates of Hell
But I won't back down."*

-Tom Petty

The friends laid in a heap of arms and limbs knotted together on the ledge, each trying their best to breathe. It took a while before one of them could move. Jefferson flipped over onto his back and let out a gasp. "What?!" he nearly screamed. Stacy and Juicebox flipped themselves over to stare at the cause of Jefferson's distress.

More impossibly high trash wall. They had only reached a plateau.

Stacy sucked in a shaky breath and had a mini breakdown. Jefferson was practically sobbing. "I can't do it guys. I'm so sorry. I can't move. Just the thought of standing, let alone climbing is making me want to jump off this ledge."

Juicebox pushed himself up with a shaky arm. "It's okay guys. It's okay." He patted his friends on their backs. "Just stay here and take a break. I have to keep going." Stacy hid her face in her hands. "No, Juice. Just wait for us please. Maybe if we rest through tonight we'll have the strength to keep going tomorrow. I just need a second to regain some strength. I—" Juicebox patted her leg and shook his head.

"Today is the day, guys. I feel it in my bones. It has to be today for me. I need to face the darkness. I need to put a stop to this." He slowly and painfully grabbed at the wall, continuing on his climb. Stacy pulled him downward. "Juicebox stop! You're not doing this alone. Let's try to pull out some of this trash to cover ourselves with for the night. We can face this together in the morning! Please!"

The mountain rumbled beneath them and shot up another dozen feet. Stacy looked away. Juicebox hopped down and wrapped his arms around her. "Hey," He made her look at him. "It's going to be okay. The mountain is growing more and more each moment. You know it and I know it. If I don't go now, it will just keep growing, making the top of it always out of reach." Stacy wiped the tears in her eyes. Jefferson sniffled next to them.

"I always knew it would just be me in the end. I think it has to be. This beast has some sort of connection with me." Stacy just shook her head. "Stacy." Juicebox tried to stop her shaking. "Stacy, you know it's true." She opened her eyes and the look in them was that of a wild woman.

"I hear him too!" She nearly yelled. Juicebox moved back from her. "What do you mean?" She tore her fingers through her hair. "I hear him. He talks to me too. It's not just you, Juicebox. You shouldn't have to face him alone. This isn't your fault. In fact, I keep wondering if maybe it's mine."

Jefferson moved closer. "Why didn't you tell us?" Stacy looked up at him miserably. "Because I didn't want you guys to know! I didn't want you to look at me differently! And honestly, I didn't want to believe it. But it's true. I hear him, which means I'm also somehow connected to him, which means

Juicebox shouldn't be facing him alone when I've got something to do with this too."

Juicebox placed his hand back on her shoulder and smiled at her. "Stacy. It's alright. There's one thing I know for sure. And that's that none of this could ever be your fault." She looked up at him with watery eyes. He continued, "I didn't tell you guys this. But the darkness told me something when we were back at that house, something that I don't think he wanted me to know." His friends were intrigued.

"He told me that he had been working on this town for a long, long time. That it was hilarious to him that I thought that I could have created him." Juicebox stared off into the wreckage of the town.

"I've got my own relationship with him. I know that for sure. And maybe you do too, Stacy. Maybe we all do. But there is no way that this is all your fault."

Stacy sniffled and looked away, still unsure. Juicebox moved a strand of electric blue hair behind her ear, bringing her eyes back to meet him.

"I've known you your whole life, Stacy Johnson. You are *light*. And light doesn't create this."

He motioned out to the horror-show of a town below them.

They stared at the wreckage in silence.

"I'm going to keep climbing." Juicebox said after a moment. "I know it's right. I know that I need to. You guys just rest and hide out. I'll be back."

He stood and grabbed a hold of the wall, securing his foot to push upward when a loud crack sounded through the mountain. In less than a second the wall crumbled beneath him. "JUICEBOX!!!!" Stacy and Jefferson screamed as he fell into a black abyss within the mountain.

Air rushed past him as he fell for what felt like a lifetime. *This must be the end.* He thought to himself when suddenly… Thud! Shlooop! He hit a soft goopy ledge of purple slime. Thud! Then another. Slurp! And another! Each slimy impact slowed his descent. With a splat he landed in a squishy pool of goo. He moved to stand and felt the tension of the warm slime sticking to him. He took goopy step after goopy step to try to move to investigate his surroundings.

He could see that he was in a dark cavern that looked as if it connected to a hallway that led deeper and deeper into the mountain. Every surface was covered with the purply ooze which seemed to be flowing and dripping from somewhere above. Juicebox stepped out of the pool and tried to make sense of which way he should go next within this cave he found himself in.

*"THIS WAY,"* a hissing voice sounded, beckoning him to follow. *"COME TO ME."* Taking a deep breath, Juicebox stepped into the cavernous hall. The air was layered in a thick musty scent, and a chill ran down his spine as if the very essence of despair lingered in the shadows. Pain panged through his gut as he continued forward.

The cave grew darker with every step he took and the walls seemed to close in around him, whispering echoes of doubt into his ears. *ALONE AGAIN.* They whispered. *ALONE FOREVER.* He knew it was the darkness and did his best to shut out the evil whispers, which proved to be difficult as he walked the eerie, unknown path.

A gentle breeze blew at his cheek and he searched for its source. He found a door-like opening just up ahead and walked toward it, the darkness intensifying the further he ventured. It swirled around him like a malevolent mist, suffocating his every breath. His heart raced and the pain in his stomach panged violently. "AH!" His knees hit the ground as he clutched to his stomach. *"YOU CAN STAY HERE."* The voice whispered to him. Juicebox shook his head and took a shaky step up to stand. "No." He whispered under his breath. He was determined to face this thing.

He walked forward and the fleshy floor sloped down into a winding path. Carefully, he sidestepped his way down until the path became so slick and steep, he was forced to slide down the narrow passageway. He screamed as he gripped around for something to hold onto to stop his fall, but it was useless. The floor was too slippery and wet. Eventually he popped out of the passageway and rolled into a landing that stood in front of a massive open cavern.

The landing extended into a ridged cliff that overlooked an endless black abyss. Juicebox crawled to the edge to peer downward. There was nowhere else to go. The shadowy abyss swirled before his eyes, taking the mountainous shape of the darkness. It oozed and dripped and loomed before him, its pink glowing eyes blinked as its sharp smile protruded forward.

"SO, YOU MADE IT..." The darkness bellowed. "I'M FLATTERED THAT YOU TRAVELED ALL THIS WAY JUST TO SEE LITTLE OL' ME." Juicebox snickered at it, disgusted. The darkness boomed and grew twenty stories higher, arching menacingly over him.

"SO, TELL ME NOW. WHAT IS IT YOU'D LIKE TO DO NOW THAT YOU'RE HERE? WE CAN PLAY A GAME? PERHAPS MY FAVORITE?" It bounded downward, its giant mouth snapping right in front of Juicebox's face. Juicebox lunged back, away from the beast.

"THIS ONE IS CALLED, 'HOW MANY TIMES HAS JUICEBOX SCREWED UP?'"

Suddenly images danced through Juicebox's mind—memories of every mistake he had ever made. Every rude name he had called someone, every failed test, every fist fight—he saw them all, one after another in living color. His mother's tears, his father's disappointment, his teachers' disdain… Juicebox clutched his hands to his head. "STOPPPPP!!!!" He yelled back at the darkness. It laughed at him.

*"THIS IS WHAT I'VE BEEN TRYING TO TELL YOU, JUICEBOX."* The darkness sneered. *"THERE IS NO WORLD IN WHICH I STOP."* Its long, crooked arms smacked the ledge where Juicebox stood. *"YOU CANNOT ESCAPE ME. I AM AND ALWAYS WILL BE YOUR CONSTANT COMPANION."* It spat the words in Juicebox's face.

"No," Juicebox shook his head at the monster. "I refuse to be consumed by you! I am more than my worst moments. I am stronger than you think!" He took a shaking breath. "I used to be afraid of you."

The darkness exploded with laughter leaning in toward the boy on the edge of the cliff. *"AND YOU AREN'T NOW!?"* It heaved as it chuckled. *"YOU ARE SHAKING, BOY. YOU CAN'T LIE TO ME. I SEE STRAIGHT THROUGH YOU."*

Juicebox shook his head. "You have no power over me." A peaceful confidence filled his voice.

The darkness leaned its jagged teeth close enough to snap Juicebox in half. *"I HAVE ALL POWER OVER YOU."* Its glowing eyes blared. *"I DECIDE EVERYTHING! WHETHER YOU EAT, WHETHER YOU SLEEP, WHETHER OR NOT YOU GET UP IN THE MORNING..."* Its voice trailed off. *"IT IS ME WHO DECIDES WHETHER OR NOT YOU FEEL ANYTHING AT ALL."* It whispered the sentence to Juicebox, its putrid breath stinging at his nose.

"No, you don't!" Juicebox shouted back. "I decided that you don't." He didn't back away from the beast as it opened its giant mouth to laugh again. *"YOU THINK YOU'RE SO SMART. BUT YOU DON'T UNDERSTAND. YOU'LL NEVER GET RID OF ME."* A huge claw-like hand rose up from the abyss and flicked Juicebox backward, sending him smashing into the wall. He lay on the ground wincing from the pain of his fresh black eye and bleeding mouth.

Pushing himself to his hands and knees, he let the blood from his mouth drip freely to the ground. "You're right." He said as he slowly moved to stand, limping to the edge of the cliff. "You will always be there. But I am in control! I choose whether or not I give your words power! I don't have to listen to you. You might be there knocking at the door, but I never, EVER, have to let you in!"

The darkness scoffed at him. *"SILLY BOY, THAT'S NOT..."* "Stop!" Juicebox cut the monster off. "I don't have to listen to you ever again! Now give me back my life!" The darkness recoiled, its form writhing in frustration. It lunged toward Juicebox, but he dodged its grasp, his willpower propelling him forward. With each step, he felt a surge of resilience, a flicker of hope that ignited within him. The darkness seethed and shrieked, unable to comprehend the strength he possessed. Summoning every ounce of courage he possessed, Juicebox took a step forward. The darkness churned and swirled, threatening to swallow him whole. But Juicebox stood his ground, staring into its abyss, and made a choice—Juicebox ran. He ran straight toward the darkness.

Reaching the end of the cliff, Juicebox leaped into the air, screaming, with his fist raised high as he lunged at the beast. The darkness flew forward with an open mouth and Juicebox dove in headfirst.

Suddenly, everything faded away.

# Chapter 17

*"Hope" is the thing with feathers–*
*That perches in the soul –*
*And sings the tune without the words –*
*And never stops – at all– ...*
*I've heard it in the chillest land –*
*And on the strangest Sea –*
*Yet – never – in Extremity,*
*It asked a crumb of me.*

*-Emily Dickinson*

Juicebox felt a rush of wind and the sensation of falling. His body trembled with fear, yet somewhere deep within him, a glimmer of hope remained. When he opened his eyes, he found himself standing in a blank white room. Before him stood a gray version of himself, devoid of color except for its pink glowing eyes. The gray figure regarded him with a solemn expression.

"*You made it.*"

Juicebox approached the figure and stared at it, confused.

"Are you... me?" He reached out to touch it. It felt like ice and he tore his hand away.

"*In a way.*" It replied, "*I'm part of you.*"

Juicebox stared at the figure, feeling completely confused, then looked around. The room seemed to be infinite.

"What is this place? Am I dead?"

Ghostlike figures of his mom and dad emerged and placed their arms around the gray Juicebox. "Mom?! Dad?!" Juicebox could feel his eyes welling up with tears at the sight of them. "Are they really— Are they real?" Juicebox could barely get the words out.

"*Yes, well... they are real memories. They live here with me.*" Video-like memories of his parents started to play out on the walls of his mind, like giant movie theater screens. Juicebox focused on a memory of his dad playing with him when he was a little kid.

They were laughing together as they played games on the living room floor. He saw another memory of his mom going out to take care of the chickens in their backyard, tossing seeds at Juicebox's feet to make the chickens run toward him.

Tears streamed down Juicebox's face. "I miss them so much." His mind turned toward their accident and whispers from the darkness began to echo in the room. *"ALL YOUR FAULT..."*

The other Juicebox began to crack and deform, bending and stretching as the form of the darkness tried to rip from him like that night in the bathroom. Juicebox jumped back with fear.

The ghosts of Juicebox's parents gently caressed the other gray Juicebox's back, speaking calm words into his ears. Juicebox tried to calm himself in the face of the chaos, noticing that as he did, the darkness faded away and the voices stopped. Other Juicebox returned to normal.

Juicebox stared in confusion. Gray Juicebox stepped forward. *"It's okay to miss them. It's okay to be sad. But you can't let go of the control. It's like driving a car. You can't let the darkness take hold of the wheel.*" Juicebox nodded but huffed a bit at the censure he was receiving. "My parents died! Not even that long ago! Of course, I'm going to lose a little control."

The other Juicebox slowly shook his head. *"You lost control way before that. Maybe you hadn't noticed but you were giving into him everyday. You listened to every word he said. It makes it harder for us, Juicebox. Harder to do well in school, harder to have friends, harder for us to get out of bed in the morning. We didn't have a choice in losing our parents… but we do have a choice in not losing ourselves."*

Juicebox nodded. He was right. "I told the darkness I was done listening to him. Done giving into his words. But I'm scared that I won't always have the strength. Especially when it's all I hear day in and day out." He breathed in deeply. "I need a plan. I need something I can do to get rid of him for good."

Gray Juicebox stepped forward. *"You can't get rid of him. There's a really strong possibility that he will never fully go away. But there are things you can do to help yourself not give in to his lies."* Juicebox rubbed at the bridge of his nose. The thought of this beast haunting him till the end of his days was overwhelming. "I always hear his voice."

"*And you always will.*"

"So, what do I do?!"

Gray Juicebox stepped forward again.

"*Stop listening to him. Stop giving his words power.*"

Juicebox moaned with frustration, burying his face in his hands. "I know! I'm just scared. I'm scared that it will wear on me every day. I'm scared I'll give into him. I need a plan. I need *something*."

Gray Juicebox nodded. "*You need to listen to the other voices.*"

Juicebox looked up. "Other voices? I've never heard any other voices?"

Gray Juicebox looked up at the ghostly figures of Mom and Dad.

"*They are smaller. Quieter. They take some effort to hear.*"

"I don't understand."

Ghost Mom and Dad walked forward and knelt next to Juicebox.

"*You are loved, Juicebox.*" His mom whispered into his ear as she kissed his cheek. "*You are kind, Juicebox.*" His dad wrapped a hand around his shoulder.

Their voices were so quiet, lower than a whisper. Tears welled in Juicebox's eyes.

"But my parents are gone. None of this is even real…"

Gray Juicebox cocked an eyebrow at him. "*Not real?*"

Juicebox felt distressed. "No! You said this was all in my mind… none of this is real." Ghost Mom and Dad rubbed his shoulders, trying to calm him down.

"*Is the darkness real then?*"

Juicebox pondered the question.

"Yes. He is very real."

"*Is he not also in your mind?*"

Juicebox nodded.

"*All of it is real, Juicebox. All of it.*"

Juicebox sat on the floor to think. His parents sat beside him.

"The other voices are all around you. They can come from many different places. Sometimes it's the voice of a loved one offering help or words of encouragement. Sometimes it's a voice from within pleading that we hang on just a little bit longer because we know deep down that help will come. Sometimes it's the stillness of the air, or the sun dancing on our skin. Sometimes it's the voice of tomorrow promising new beginnings. These voices stick around to look after us, to protect us from the darkness. They are always there. But we have to choose to listen."

Juicebox nodded. His mother took his hand and his mind flashed to the outside world and the wreckage of the town that he still didn't know how to fix.

"But the darkness has spread so far… if he's not gone for good now, I don't know how we are going to fix this mess. How are we going to heal the people and rebuild the town?"

His mother spoke to him now. "The darkness is often contagious. It spreads and spreads and spreads its shadow all over. But light chases out *darkness, Juicebox—and it is contagious as well. Believe that it will get better. Believe that it's going to be okay. Help who you can and choose to listen to the right voices."* Juicebox hugged her tightly. "Do what I know first." His mother smiled at him. *"Exactly. And then keep going."*

She turned to Gray Juicebox and motioned him toward them. Gray Juicebox knelt down and joined himself to Juicebox, seeping into him like water into grass—the two becoming one. His parents hugged him tightly and he smiled at the warmth he felt from their embrace. A hope bloomed in his chest, stronger and brighter than anything he had felt in a long, long time. He closed his eyes and the world around him drifted away.

# Chapter 18

*"When it is dark enough, you can see the stars."*

-Ralph Waldo Emerson

Juicebox woke up and found himself lying atop a sticky heap of trash. He stared up into the sky. It was *blue*! A deep, darkening blue—the sun was fading from the sky... but still! It was blue! Birds fluttered above. He rolled himself off of the heap and took in a deep breath. The air felt so different than it did just a few hours ago. It felt so fresh and clean and new. Juicebox turned himself around to get a good look at his surroundings.

The monstrous mountain of pulsing flesh was gone. In its place stood a dump-sized stretch of waste and debris. It looked as if a meteor made of garbage had hit the town and left a trashy slime filled crater in its place. The town was definitely going to need some cleaning up. It was going to need a lot of things… but Juicebox could tell that something had changed.

He searched around for monsters but couldn't see any. Instead, weary townspeople shuffled around in a confused daze. Some were hugging and celebrating tiredly. They were all coming back to themselves again.

"Juicebox!" he heard his name being called in the distance. "Hey Juicebox, over here!" He heard them yell again. Juicebox looked to his right and saw his two best friends, Stacy and Jefferson running over to where he stood. "There you are!" They both crushed him into a hug and the three friends squeezed each other tighter than ever. "Did you notice the sky?" Stacy jumped up and down excitedly. "It's blue!!!" She squealed. "It's finally blue again!" Juicebox laughed. "I saw it. It just wasn't quite my favorite shade." He flicked his eyes to her hair. She threw her arms around him again and kissed his cheek. Jefferson chuckled beside them.

"You did it, man." He patted Juicebox on the back. "I don't know what you did inside that mountain—I don't know how you *survived* inside that mountain. But you freaking did it, dude. Everything is going back to normal." Juicebox smiled and stared at the scene around him once more.

The sun had gone down now, and stars were making their way across the sky. Each little light sparkled and danced and the moon rose big and bright and full. The beauty of what was once so common caught the eyes of everyone around them, and they all stared up together at the sight. The lights seemed to shine down on each of them. Illuminating each face with a heavenly glow. Juicebox remembered his mother and listened carefully to the gentle breeze blowing in the night air. He could have sworn that he heard an, *I love you.*

He closed his eyes and focused on the voice. It was warm and encouraging. He decided it was real.

Stacy grabbed his and Jefferson's hands and squeezed.

"What do you guys say we have one more sleepover tonight?" They walked forward together, hand in hand.

Somehow, despite all the walking, running and climbing they had done over the past three days, the moonlit walk was refreshing. Trash and debris still covered everything, but a new beauty hung in the air, and the friends each felt confident in their hearts that things would be put back together again now.

They hiked their way back to Juicebox's grandma's house. Stacy peeked her head through the window of her own house on the way. "Mom's fine." She said, turning back toward her friends. "Snuggled up the couch with this month's boyfriend." She rolled her eyes and Juicebox draped his arm around her shoulder. "I'm sorry, Stace." She leaned her head onto his shoulder as they walked. "You know you can always talk to us about that… we know it's hard for you." Stacy smiled up at him. "I know."

Jefferson took a moment to check on his parents as well. Stacy and Juicebox followed him through his mangled front door. "Mom? Dad? He called out hesitantly. His parents emerged from the kitchen, rushing toward Jefferson with relief as they pulled him in for an embrace. Stacy and Juicebox walked back outside to give them some privacy. Jefferson emerged a few minutes later, wiping at the tears on his face. "I'm so glad they're okay." He sucked in a sob. "We are too, buddy." Stacy and Juicebox hugged him tightly. "Do you want to stay behind with them tonight?" Juicebox asked. Jefferson shook his head. "The house isn't safe right now. They told me to go on ahead and stay with you guys somewhere that isn't torn to shreds. I'll see them tomorrow."

They finally made it to Juicebox's grandma's house. Somehow it had survived the craziness, and a tiny light shone through the front window. Juicebox twisted the doorknob and peered inside. The TV was on in the living room. Grandma's slippered feet were peeking out from behind the wall, propped up on her recliner.

"Grandma?" He called out. "In here, kid." She held a cigarette to her mouth and puffed on it sleepily. "Come on in and sit down. I was just about to head to bed. You lot can put on a movie." She heaved herself out of her chair and shuffled down the hall to her room. "Grandma, wait!" Juicebox called out. She turned back to face him. "Are you okay? Have you been alright these past few days?" Grandma chuckled. "Of course! I mean it would have been nice if you called... but I was just happy you were finally out of the house, playing with your friends."

She turned back around and shuffled off to bed. Juicebox turned to his friends with widened eyes. Jefferson's mouth hung open in shock. "I told you guys she wouldn't even notice the apocalypse if it came knocking on her door!" They all busted up laughing in utter disbelief.

"Good for Grandma." Stacy smiled. "I like a woman who doesn't let anything get her down."

The three friends considered putting on a movie, but all Juicebox had were monster films, and they were all monstered out. Exhausted, they moved to set up camp in Juicebox's room. When Juicebox opened his door he felt a pang of homesickness. He had never realized it before but he missed his old room. His *swamp.* He glanced at all of the boxes still cluttering the room, filled with his mom's old things. He closed his eyes and listened for another voice. "*Make it your own,*" it whispered to him gently. He put the thought to the side. With time, this room would feel like home. Swamp 2.0.

Stacy took the bed and Juicebox and Jefferson layered blankets and pillows on the floor beside each other. They flicked off the lights and snuggled into what felt like luxury after their hectic adventure. Silence stole the room but Juicebox stared at the ceiling. He gazed at the retro glow in the dark stars that his mother had pasted to the ceiling as a child and thought of the beauty of that night's sky again.

"Juicebox. What happened out there?" Stacy turned over in the bed to look down at him. "How did you do it? How did you conquer the darkness?"

"I don't think I really did." He admitted. His friends listened closely.

"I found him in the heart of that mountain. I faced off with him and told him that he didn't have any power over me—that I didn't have to listen to him. I stormed at him and he swallowed me whole." Juicebox paused. "I don't really know what happened to him after that. If I had to guess, I'd say he's still here. I think he always will be."

Jefferson made a nervous sound beside him.

"But I know now what he is. I decided what he is to me."

"What is he, Juice?" Stacy prodded.

Juicebox placed his hands behind his head, still staring up at the stars.

"He's just a voice inside my head. One of many. And I get to choose which ones I listen to. I get to choose what I believe."

Juicebox turned to stare up at Stacy. "And so do you, Stace."

She nodded at him. "You might have to teach me."

Juicebox put a hand on Jefferson's shoulder and smiled at his friends. "We'll all have to teach each other."

He stared at the glow in the dark stars as sleep began to take him, imagining himself riding on their tails as he shot through the sky. The dark vastness of space trailed behind and loomed above him, but he rode forward like a pirate through the sea of lights. *I am a warrior of my own mind.* He thought to himself. *The captain of my own life.*

It felt like a relief in a way, to know that the darkness would remain. To know that more than anything, the darkness signaled to him parts of himself that needed compassion and healing. It calmed him to know that though it was as vast as the infinite midnight sky, that he had the capacity to hold it, and still move forward—that he was somehow bigger than the biggest monster he could have ever imagined possible.

*Unwavering.*

*Tenacious.*

*Resilient.*

These were words he would have never used to describe himself just a few days ago, yet now they coursed through his mind like a river of light. He decided he would hold on to them.

¤¤¤

That night Juicebox dreamed of sunshine. It spread on his skin and filled him with warmth. He bathed in it, basked in it, ran through its beams until he couldn't run anymore. His parents ran with him, side by side, as real, tangible, and comforting as they had ever been before. The three of them held each other in the light.

He awoke to the smell of cinnamon pancakes.

# Acknowledgments

This project has been my passion for nearly the last decade of my life. As one could imagine, it's passed through the ears of nearly all of my loved ones, and received so much support from the people that are nearest and dearest to my heart. I would like to thank everyone that had a part in bringing this story to life.

To my beautiful and fantastical wife, Skye, thank you so much for all your writing support and the many late nights discussing this idea. You have believed and encouraged me on this project for more than eight years now. Saggy Town wouldn't exist without you.

To both my parents, thank you so much for all of your unending patience and encouragement throughout the years. And especially to my mom, Kimberly Staker, thank you for the countless hours of writing support, editing and idea bouncing. This story wouldn't exist the same way without your involvement.

A huge thank you to Airon Pritt, Shelley Betker, and Ashley Betker, for all being the first readers of the book and for your very helpful feedback. Your brilliant minds found the problems that I was too blind to see and helped immensely in bringing the story together more fully.

To the awe-inspiring Aaron Conley, thank you for your incredible help bringing this story to life through illustration. Your knowledge and experience were an incredible asset on this project as well as your personal taste and style. Your work played an enormous role in developing this world and bringing this story to life.

To Jared Morgan, thank you from the bottom of my heart for believing in this story so much as to invest in the project and lending your continued support throughout its creation. I am so grateful for all that you have done and am very blessed to have you on this journey with me.

To Tim Schulte, my editor extraordinaire. Thank you for all of the phone calls, advice, and hard work. Your wisdom and expertise helped bring this story to the next level and I appreciate you so much.

To all my supporters who have followed along my journey online, thank you so much for your love and encouragement. It was your support for my illustrations, and love of the world of Saggy Town that gave me the courage to continue to pursue this idea through the years.

And finally, to John Taylor, my business partner and friend. Before you came along, Saggy Town was just an idea. An idea that might not have ever been anything. You provided the opportunity to bring this story to life — not only for me, for you, and for those we know, but you also gave this story the potential to be heard by people all around the world. From the late-night calls discussing the story to reviewing illustrations and encouraging me through the stress and struggles that have come along the way, this book has become intertwined and mixed with bits of you. I can confidently say this book would not have ever existed without you.

# About The Author

Caleb Staker is a character designer and storyboard artist currently working in the animation industry. He loves to work on dark and whimsical projects and has a particular interest in all things related to the stop motion animation world. Caleb has worked on a number of notable productions for companies such as Warner Animation Group, Disney+, ShadowMachine, and more—but hopes to one day bring Saggy Town to life as a feature film or limited series show. He and his beautiful wife, Skye, and their two little ones, Violet and Leonardo, live in sunny Las Vegas, Nevada where they enjoy bingeing fantasy tv shows and encouraging each other's wild ideas as they dream of their happily ever after. You can visit Caleb online at Instagram: @calebstaker and Website: calebstakerart.com

Made in the USA
Las Vegas, NV
20 January 2024

84643695R00204